Tantalizing

20

SHORT
STORIES

By LAWRENCE GRABER

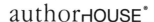

authorHOUSE®

AuthorHouse™
1663 Liberty Drive
Bloomington, IN 47403
www.authorhouse.com
Phone: 1 (800) 839-8640

Published by AuthorHouse 04/08/2016

ISBN: 978-1-5049-8402-7 (sc)
ISBN: 978-1-5049-8401-0 (e)

Library of Congress Control Number: 2016903717

❖❖❖❖ CONTENTS ❖❖❖❖

❖❖❖❖❖❖❖❖❖❖❖❖❖

IMPROBABLE COINCIDENCE

It was dusk. The remnants of an unusually dense, foggy afternoon remained. Doctor Peter Rubin found himself in the County Hospital parking lot after a grueling ten hours of surgical procedures brought about by a series of automobile accidents, the result of the murky weather conditions.

Fighting fatigue, he held the doorhandle of the Chevy several seconds before entering. He seated himself, folding his hands on his lap for a moment, but soon after turned the key and with the engine purring, savored the restful atmosphere.

After collecting himself, he left the parking area and was soon in the midst of the ongoing traffic. With his mind clouded with thoughts of the severe injuries incurred by those unfortunate patients, and unmindful of the dusk and still remaining areas of fog, Peter was not keeping pace with his everyday safe driving habits.

At seventy miles per hour, he entered the ramp leading to the parkway without his usual cautious approach into the high speed zone when merging with parkway traffic.

Too fast! Too fast! Too close! Too close! Peter severely miscalculated the merge sending his Chevy into the path of an SUV, flinging it upside down, through the air, just clearing the head of Cody Whitmore running along the bikepath lining the parkway. Avoiding a life-threatening encounter, Cody threw himself to the ground, instinctively using his arms to cover his face. The SUV's impact tore apart the front end of the vehicle. Sparks from the smash-up instantly ignited the fire beginning to engulf the interior of the Chevy. With fast-moving flames closing in on the victim, Cody, in a controlled panic, decided immediately on a rescue attempt.

"Jesus, how do I get this guy out of there?"

Peter, with his heavy frame, was not easily extricated. The overturned Chevy required Cody to bend on his knees, reach into the cab with his other hand braced against the door frame, avoid the nearby flames, grab the doctor's pants belt, and with great heft succeeded in pulling him from the mangled metal. Bits of his clothing still afire, his hair singed, his left cheek seared, Peter was sprawled on the concrete bikepath. Cody, his fingers slightly blistered from the heat, was still able to remove his tee shirt and smother the flames smoldering on the unconscious doctor's clothing. Then, mindful of a potential explosion, quickly dragged the victim several feet onto a grassy area. Seconds later the Chevy, now totally engulfed with flame, was shattered by the explosive force.

Still unable to calm himself from the near fatal incident, together with his gut-wrenching rescue, Cody sat himself near the unconscious Peter, his outstretched arms resting on his folded knees, gazing ahead, not seeing anything, unable to believe what he had just endured; then, with trembling hands, he used his phone to contact 911. With what appeared to be minutes, fire department and police units arrived, quickly dousing the flames of the burning Chevy, while a medical team evaluated and attended to the doctor's injuries.

Scores of other runners gathered, encircling Cody who remained close by in the event his personal account was asked for, but with other obvious priorities at the scene, and little attention paid to his heroics, Cody soon continued his run on the bikepath, nonetheless pleased with himself for what he had accomplished.

With the situation under control, and Peter being wheeled to a waiting ambulance, a fireman asked, eyeing the crowd, "Hey, who pulled this guy out from the wreck. Anybody see him?"

Upon arriving home, Cody immediately phoned his parents to make them aware of his excruciating experience and to assure them, if they read any news account, that, except for his slightly blistered fingers, he was physically fine.

The following morning, The Portland Courier, delivered daily to his front porch was waiting for Cody. Evidently personnel from the news media arrived after Cody's departure. One paragraph on the inside column covering the accident, questioned the whereabouts of the stranger, who, at his own risk, saved Doctor Peter Rubin's life.

Noting from the report that Doctor Rubin was being treated at the County Hospital, Cody and his proud parents decided to visit him and to introduce and identify their son as the young hero.

With most of his upper torso and face swathed in bandages, his leg in traction, Peter, although in great pain, received the Whitmore family.

"Hello Doctor Rubin. Hope we're not intruding. We are Emma and Ryan Whitmore and this is my son Cody." After wishing him well and with hopes that he soon return to his medical practice, the subject soon centered on the tragic circumstances of the near fatal encounter.

"Fortunately Cody was there at the right time and the right place, although not at his own pleasure, for him to rescue you."

"Cody, thank you for visiting and thank you for my life. You'll always be my hero."

Doctor Rubin: "Whitmore. Whitmore. Now why does that name ring a bell? Many years ago, practicing at a pediatric section in a Boston Hospital, my colleagues and I were constantly at the side of a severely premature newborn. The prognosis was dim, with little chance for survival. Over a period of months of particularly intensive attention, our team persevered and the child was able to leave in the hands of this very grateful mother."

"Doctor Peter Rubin! Doctor Peter Rubin! Now I remember that name! Oh my god!, Oh my god! You were there for our son."

Yes... Doctor Peter Rubin was there, although not at his own pleasure, at the right time and the right place, for his rescue of Cody Whitmore.

A SHORT VISIT

❖ ❖ ❖ ❖ ❖ ❖ ❖ ❖ ❖ ❖ ❖ ❖ ❖

The door to apartment 2E was slightly open. Jason said it would be when I called him on the lobby intercom.

He always said, "If you're in the neighborhood, come up and say "hello", but please call before and give me about fifteen minutes to get dressed." I did.

"Don't be shocked when you see me. My beautiful red hair is gone. It's that damn chemotherapy. And if I suddenly stop talking, it's because of this stupid thing I have growing in my brain. It tells me when I can talk and when I can't. Very frustrating... very depressing… especially for a guy like me. I like to communicate."

Jason welcomed me without getting up. He looked small, sitting centered on the sofa. The oversized provincial furniture, his loss of hair and a great amount of bodyweight took me back somewhat. I had never been to his apartment and hadn't seen him for some time. Everything seemed strange; the atmosphere close.

"Coralynne should be back soon. She's out shopping. She'll be happy to see you."

Jason suggested that I sit in the wing chair closest to him. "So what's happening with you?" he asked, getting himself more comfortable. "Still doing drawings like you did when you were a kid?"

"Well somewhat. I'm an art director for a few newsstand magazines. If I want to be fancy, I call myself a graphic designer." He laughed. We always enjoyed each other's humor no matter how bad.

"So tell me, how's the family? Paula, Evelyn? Everything's O.K.? Your children?" Jason seemed hungry for news.

"Everything's O.K. You know my mother's expecting her eighth great grandchild."

"That's really something. I'll bet your dad would be proud if he could see the family now."

"He'd be taking tons of photos. You know my father was the family camera buff. He had that old Kodak that he treasured… remember?…with bellows?"

"I know the one you mean," said Jason looking back. "You looked down into the eyepiece and shielded the sun with your palm. It was postcard size. Right?"

"Right," I agreed. "And do you remember the giant Lilac bush we had in our backyard?"

"Sure I do. He almost always used it as a backdrop, lining us up, tall at the back, short in the front, like a school graduation photo." We both smiled, recalling how my dad measured us back to back to see who was taller.

"Know what I remember best?" I asked. "In some photos the only thing in focus was the Lilac bush." More smiles. "I still have a picture where you were in the back row with me in the front next to Greta and the two Normans. I must have been five years old. Damn. I should have brought it today. There's also a shot of you and my brother Irv, squaring off like fighters in a boxing ring."

The mention of Irv quickly brought us from nostalgia to reality. "That Irv." Jason looked up at an imaginary spot on the ceiling, drawing the tips of his fingers across his mouth. "He was something else. I never told you how he…

Jason struggled for words, nothing coming from his mouth. It was that stupid thing growing in his brain. He warned me about it. A slight embarrassed smile crossed his face. We stared at each other for a minute or so…waiting…still nothing.

Carolynne came through the front door carrying loaded bags from her food shopping. "Larry, what a surprise! So nice to see you." We kissed and I helped carry the bags into the kitchen.

"I was in the neighborhood and decided to say "hello" to you and Jason. Hope I'm not intruding."

"Of course not. Would you like some coffee?"

"Yes, if Jason will join me."

"I was just beginning to tell Larry the story of his brother, Doctor Irv," said Jason, "the one he told us to keep confidential. I guess we can tell Larry. It happened so long ago."

"Go ahead," nodded Coralynne.

"Anyway, my son Robert, who now lives in California, had Polio when he was a youngster. Your brother came to see him in the hospital every single day from New Jersey. You hear that? Every single day! He kept our spirits up. After all, we were dealing with strange doctors and nurses and Robert was only six years old. I think we would have caved in without Irv. He was our God." Tears welled in his eyes. "A great guy… I'll never forget him."

"How long has he been gone?" Coralynne asked, folding a shopping bag.

"Twenty-four years." Jason wiped another tear. "And did you know my brother and Sylvia were grandparents seven times after he passed away."

"Too bad." Carolynne shook her head. "He would have liked that."

"And two of his children married Christians. Can you imagine what would happen if your dad and mine, Jason, our orthodox fathers, would wake up and see how many of their children married 'goyim'?… Oh my god! I forgot! You married Coralynne! I'm so sorry."

"That's all right," Coralynne and Jason assured me almost simultaneously.

To curb my embarrassment I quickly changed the course of our conversation.

"You met Coralynne when you were stationed in North Carolina, didn't you?"

"Yes, but we didn't start our lives together until I returned from overseas."

"With a Distinguished Flying Cross. Right?"

"Let's not talk about that. It's not important anymore."

"We've had a good life together, Jason and me," added Coralynne, "despite our different religions."

"What would I do without her?" whispered Jason, looking at Coralynne busy at the refrigerator. "Especially now."

Our meeting was getting a bit heavy so I decided to cut out. I stood up from the wing chair and straightened myself. "Well, this graphic designer has to get going. You know, back to the old drawing board."

Jason grinned. Another bad joke. Coralynne came into the living room. I kissed her and took a rain check on the coffee.

"Visit us again soon, Larry."

"Yeah…So long…"

Jason was still sitting in the center of the sofa. He thanked me for coming. I bent down and kissed his wet cheek. We both knew I would never see him again.

REFLECTIONS OF THE
GREAT DEPRESSION
❖ ❖ ❖ ❖ ❖ ❖ ❖ ❖ ❖ ❖ ❖ ❖ ❖ ❖ ❖ ❖

It was the year 1932. And there they were. Two youngsters, perhaps seven or eight years old, a bit disheveled and without shoes or socks. As they approached, Mrs. Schmulovitz, a good samaritan proprietor of the local candy store, told them to wait. Inside she went and returned with two thick slabs of fresh rye bread smothered with butter. A polite "Thank you" from the youngsters and away they went, devouring their appreciated, infrequent meal.

Food lines sprung up here and there with many on the line bedraggled, along with some well-dressed, a throwback when adequate income allowed for proper business attire. Teachers appeared to be the only ones with steady although modest incomes. Only one teacher at my grade school drove a car.

In that same candy store you were able to buy a cigarette for one penny. Fifteen cents for a pack of twenty cigarettes was far too expensive for the average smoker. By selling one cigarette for a penny, the owner of the store gained an additional five cents profit on every fifteen cent pack of twenty cigarettes.

Across the street from the candy store was a shoe mart frequented by my family for many years. After one year of wear, our worn out scuffed shoes were discarded. Popular at that time for my siblings and me were the most expensive of the store's limited selection: Buster Browns or Thom McCans at $3.50 a pair. Dad always bought the best for us.

A short walk and we were part of a small congregation gathered to witness a spectacular event: Television! The manager of the radio store was displaying a not-yet-for sale twelve inch circular television in the large window facing the avenue. For the group, staring in awe at the scratchy almost non-descernable images, it was a thrilling event. A far cry from the family huddling around our small Philco radio in the evening, listening to President Roosevelt's 'Fireside Chat' or the Jack Benny comedy hour sponsored by Jello pudding.

I remember walking with my six year old brother past that candy store on the way to the theatre one Saturday morning. In my pocket was a dime each for the tickets and one penny for candy. Inadvertently, one dime was spent for the penny candy. I explained the dilemma at the ticket window. The attendant, looking down at my six year old brother, "Don't cry little boy. For your one dime you can both go inside and see the movies. They're also a lot of comedies showing today. Enjoy!"

A short trolley ride and we were at my aunt and uncle's family grocery. After school, located nearby, I delivered, by hand, food stuff ordered mostly by the elderly. Average tip for the five or six block trek was five cents. You hear that! One nickel! I also remember helping my uncle set up a window display of his products on sale. In the center of the group were corn flake boxes arranged in a pyramid. A price tag at the top of the pyramid read: Thirteen cents. Many years later I was informed that my father was helpful, during that period, by financing the purchase of some grocery shelf items to help keep the place afloat.

I always felt that my father, while a bit strict, was also fair and had a soft heart. Despite his failed, once substantial business, he still had sufficient resources to sustain my family and those of his older brothers who were experiencing difficulties during this trying period. Without their asking he volunteered to assist with the cost of rent, the shuttled coal for the basement stove, the monthly food tabs at the local butcher shop and grocery.

In another instance, smoke billowed from the windows across the street from my home. Flames followed. With the fire eventually under control, my sister asked my father if her friend from across the street could stay with us until her home was made livable. With little hesitation, my father responded. "Tell your friend that she, her brother and parents can stay with us. We have space in our attic. We'll find some cots." Followed by my mother's admonition: "Okay! Okay! But keep that woman out of my kitchen!"

Not long after that arrangement, one sunny morning, came a tap on our large kitchen window facing the backyard. Opening the back door, my mother faced a rather well-attired middle-aged man. "What can I do for you?" With his eyes staring at the ground, "I wonder if you can spare a sandwich. Anything, anything at all." After seconds sizing him up, "Okay, I'll make you a sandwich and I'll even add a cup of soup if you never come back." He finished his meal on the back steps and never came back.

Unfortunately, washers and dryers were not yet invented. On occasion, perhaps once or twice a month, the 'laundry man' would arrive on those back steps with a heavy bundle of neatly-folded laundered items. Our large family required his service to supplement washing in the large basement sink and drying on the clothes line that linked our bedroom window to the nearest telephone pole. He appreciated the two one dollar bills he received.

For those parents, intent on their children entering college, the challenge was almost overbearing. With little or no family earnings, predepression savings for tuition, now used for daily existence, quickly evaporated. Discussion at the dinner table no longer involved courses of study. College for almost all, was no longer a consideration.

In addition to the anxieties and instability in this period of time, diseases such as measles, chicken pox, diphtheria, whooping cough and others were prevalent. Doctors always came to your home with his little black bag and stethoscope. His fee, generally, if you could afford it, was $2.00. If you were unable to, the apple pie cooling on the kitchen windowsill was an acceptable payment.

At nine years of age, I could not have been aware of those prosperous years preceding the depression. With great friends and food on the table, for me, naively, it was the best of times. For those of a greater age, with meager or nonexistent income, unfortunately, it was the worst of times.

Despite the dismal circumstances the average family had to endure, there was always a bit of humor that found its way into those dark days:

Mrs. Goldberg was asked by a concerned neighbor why she appeared to be agitated.

"My husband lost his business," she answered.

"My god, how did that happen?," asked a neighbor.

"Someone jumped out of a window and landed on his pushcart!"

On occasion, my friends and I would gather near good samaritan Mrs. Schmulovitz's candy store. Hey! Free tootsyrolls are something you wouldn't want to pass up!

THE ODDS ARE WAY OFF

❖ ❖

Rick knew if he didn't move fast enough, the incoming German shell would sure as hell tear his head off. He dove headlong for the nearest crater, the explosive force catching him in midair and slamming him into the deepest part of the hole. Stunned, looking past his feet at the sky, Rick lay in the same position for several minutes except for feeling where a sliver of shrapnel ate into his brow. "Why are they shelling this goddam place. There's no goddam nothing here," he grumbled.

Annoyed at being wounded, he slapped off his helmet to examine the damage to his brow. Turning his body to raise himself, his eyes caught something protruding from the earth not three inches from his face. The close proximity preventing him getting a sharp image, he righted himself by tumbling to all fours to get a better focus on the object. "Jesus, it's someone's fingers! Who the hell is buried here? Friend…enemy? No big deal," he reasoned, staring at the bloated, pale blue flesh. "He's dead anyway." Nevertheless, Rick felt uneasy sharing the hole with a dead stranger. "Where the hell are the guys, dammit!"

All at once the shelling stopped. An eerie quiet followed. Still shaken from the blast, Rick let his backpack drop to the ground, dug the butt of his rifle into the soft earth and let himself fall against the crater wall. He opened a can of rations with his trench knife and nibbled, his eyed not leaving the pale blue flesh.

Suddenly aware that there were no sounds, no noises, he raised his head slightly above ground level and peered across the open field. His eyes squinted to cope with the snow's reflected sunlight. "Damn, we were together before this stupid shelling started. They couldn't all be dead. What the hell is going on?"

Sliding back to his original position, his eyes once again locked onto the fingertips. At the same time he mulled over whether to remain in the crater or search for his unit. The almost- buried hand and his next move equally occupying his mind, he impulsively reached over to his pack, lifted the foxhole shovel and began to push aside the earth around the swollen fingers. Startled when the shovel head hit a hard surface, he dropped the shovel and used his fingers to dust the earth where the impact occurred.

"The hand's got a ring! Hey, Joey had a ring like that…and it's got the same initial!" A nervous smile opened his lips. "I don't remember Joey's hand being that heavy. No…these aren't Joey's fingers. Besides, the odds are way off…but damn, that looks like Joey's ring and damn, that could be Joey buried there!"

Grabbing the shovel, he dug furiously, removing the earth around the forearm and higher, reaching the shoulder area in a few minutes. Rick, swallowing hard, saw that the sleeve of the battle jacket ended at the shoulder in shreds. "God, this sleeve is attached to nothing! This arm is attached to nothing!" Throwing the shovel aside and falling to his knees, Rick used both his hands to dig maniacally around the shoulder. When the resulting space confirmed that the rest of Joey was not there, Rick felt alienated, repulsed. He sat back on his rump, his bunched-up knees supporting his outstretched arms. "What if it is Joey?," he thought as he used his fingers to scrape some caked soil from his palms. "How do I leave here without knowing if it's Joey? That ring…I've got to get Joey's ring."

Unfolding his knees, he crawled the few feet to the hand. For the first time he became aware that it was an almost closed fist, grasping something that wasn't there. Holding the wrist firmly against the ground, Rick needed all of his strength to unlock the one finger bearing the ring. It didn't take him too long to realize the diameter of the band against the bloated finger made it virtually impossible to remove the ring. Rick exploded. He suddenly grabbed the elbow, lifted the arm from its grave and slammed it to the ground. Regaining his composure after staring for some time at the grisly scene, an unattached arm against the dark earth, he began to feel disgust for himself for having treated Joey that way. "I'm sorry Joey," he whispered. "Please forgive me."

With the sun down and the day's events having run him dry, Rick laid himself close to the arm. He placed his cheek on the bloated, pale blue hand, savoring the moment... and closed his eyes.

Some hours later, an exploding shell awakened him with a jolt. The voice of his sergeant shouting instructions was reassuring. Grabbing his pack and rifle, he scrambled to just below the rim and...no...he couldn't leave Joey's ring. He slid back down, unsheathed his trench knife and clenching his teeth, dismembered the finger between the ring and the knuckle of the hand. Pushing the finger into his breast pocket, he buttoned the flap for safekeeping, scampered out and rejoined his unit.

"Where the hell were you?," shouted the sergeant as they and the others ran across the pockmarked field towards a forested area. "The guys thought you got it."

"I'm O.K. I was with a friend."

"A friend?"

"Yeah. I lost a good buddy back there."

"Too bad."

Reaching the protection of the trees, the sergeant had the radio operator inform field headquarters of their position. The unit was ordered to remain there and await instructions. Touching the point of a small lead pencil to his tongue, the sergeant began to list the names of those unaccounted for and those who were surely gone. As he questioned the survivors for positive information, Rick pressed his palm to his breast pocket.

His eyes welled. "Sorry I had to do that Joey. It was the only way I could get your ring. You know I wouldn't hurt you for a million bucks. Right? You didn't have no pain anymore and so I did it. But I'm still sorry, Joey."

Rick waited for the evening darkness to have some privacy and also time to gather himself mentally to once again handle Joey's finger. He reached into the flapped pocket and finding the ring, brought out the finger with it. Easily removing the ring from the finger's severed end, Rick used the moonlight to read the inscription on the inside of the band. His pulse quickened. There it was! 'To Joseph, from Uncle Harry, 1934'. "It was Joey back there…Damn!"

The first light of day opened the sky above the trees. Rick looked at the finger lying on the ground where he placed it hours before. "I've got to bury Joey. I just can't throw him away. I've got to bury him." Using his trench knife, Rick carved a neat rectangular shape some two inches deep. Then, thinking back, a serene expression on his face, he and Joey, eight-year-olds, performed the same ritual in Joey's backyard…a dead sparrow found on the lawn…two ice cream sticks for a cross. Rick felt comfortable with the thought. Joey was alive then.

Snapping back to reality, he placed some dry grass at the bottom of the cut as a cushion, put the ring back on and laid the finger carefully in the hole, centering it; giving Joey enough room for comfort. Using the edge of his palm as a broom, he began to sweep earth into the opening. At that very moment the new sunlight sparkled a facet of the ring's initial. Rick regarded it as a signal. "Maybe from God," he thought. "Maybe the guy upstairs doesn't want me to bury Joey's ring." After some reflection, he decided that Joey's family would appreciate it's return. Removing the ring once again, he laid the finger back on the cushion, closed the hole and tamped the earth with his fist. Rick brushed the area clean, placed two twigs at right angles over the grave and crossed himself; a prayer, inaudibly, on his lips.

Rick could not contain himself as the train pulled into the rural station. The family swarmed over him with handshakes, kisses, bearhugs. Dad drove the old Chevy down Cedar Street past the elementary school where he and Joey first met.

"You know Rick," said his mother, "every one of you came back...every young man. What a blessing for the families...for the town."

Rick, stunned by the news, sat motionless, staring ahead, only able to nod his head in acknowledgement. "Joey's alive? What the hell happened back there? I know he's dead," thinking to himself as he felt Joey's ring in his breast pocket. Who the hell is this guy playing Joey? Damn!"

"And we're having a coming home party at the church hall Saturday night. What a blessing."

Mustering the courage to see if Joey was still in this world, he asked with feigned casualness, "Dad could we stop at Joey's place for a few minutes. I just want to say 'hello'. Haven't seen him for awhile."

Rick walked slowly up the concrete path to Joey's front door, his heart pounding. "Joey is dead. I buried him myself. Somebody is making a big mistake. I said a prayer over Joey. That's it. Joey is dead and buried."

Rick used the door knocker. Joey opened the door. He grabbed Rick in a handshake and pulled him into the foyer.

"Rick, how the hell are you? Everything O.K.? Not a scratch...right?"

"Right." A shocked, almost traumatized Rick could only stare at Joey, all the while not able to satisfy himself with any explanation of whom it was he apologized to, whom he agonized over...whom he buried.

After a few minutes of not assimilating anything Joey said, Rick excused himself. "I've got to get going. My family is waiting outside. See you at the party Saturday night."

"Okay. Glad you came back in one piece."

The Chevy pulled onto Rick's driveway. He remained in the car after the family walked to the white wraparound porch and waited for him. Rick, in a trance after seeing Joey, stared out at the farmland he left three years before. "Maybe I should have given Joey his ring now. Why didn't I?"

Rick nervously entered the church hall and despite the crowd, his eyes immediately caught what looked like the back of Joey. A tap on the shoulder…Joey turned around. "Hey, where's your graduation ring?" Rick asked almost immediately, not able to control his curiosity. "The one your Uncle Harry gave you."

"Oh, that…Boy, was I stupid. Needed some cash to get back into a Poker game. I planned to buy it back but the guy left for the front before payday. I really feel lousy about it."

Rick slowly unbuttoned the flap of his breast pocket and secretly closed his fist around the ring. "I've got something for you Joey. Open you hand." Rick placed the ring on Joey's palm. In shock, unbelieving and unable to contain himself, Joey examined it for the inscription on the inside of the band; 'To Joseph, from Uncle Harry, 1934'. In doing so, he became aware of some additional markings on the outside of the band; 'To Joey, Welcome Home, Your Pal Rick, 1945'. Joey grabbed Rick in a bearhug and with tears welling in his eyes asked, "Where the hell did you get this Rick?"

"Well…I'll tell you," Rick began slowly. "It was at the Battle of the Bulge. This damn shell was coming straight for me, sure as hell going to tear my head off."

NEVER AGAIN

❖ ❖ ❖ ❖ ❖ ❖ ❖ ❖ ❖ ❖ ❖

Mark's eyes immediately spotted the glaring front page headline of the local newspaper, 'The Citizen', lying face up, delivered daily to his front porch.

The headline, 'Bank Heists At Alarming Rate', was set in king-size type.

Columns on pages two and three were consumed with details of the latest event along with the fact that six heists in the county were accomplished in the past eight months.

Mark thought it was incredible that the heists were carried out apparently by a single thief, a conclusion based on the descriptions from the various tellers who were approached with the usual threatening note. All confirmed: "About five feet, nine inches tall, white male, dark hair, gaunt features, dark clothing, walked with an apparent limp."

"I bet I could do a heist," Mark thought as he poured through the report. "It seems really easy. Write a threatening note, ask for cash and leave. Simple! I'd like to try that some day."

As the months passed, Mark could not dispel the thought that he could very well carry out a heist. Soon he found himself composing threatening notes, rephrasing them several times and eventually tossing them in the wastebasket. Nevertheless, he soon was obsessed with the thought and actually planned to follow through.

Serious consideration followed. Surely 'write a note, ask for cash and leave' was a bit naive. There had to be a blueprint, a specific approach, a modus operandi.

Mark, remembering the coverage of the heist, compiled a list of apparent strategies used by the thief and added some of his own as a base for his plan of action. For instance: time of day (crowds could help cover his getaway), type of clothing (something difficult to describe), nonchalance (wait in line with other customers), fleeing on foot (a licenseplate could be his downfall) and finally, a threatening note to the teller, written with computer-generated type ("I have a gun, stay calm, stuff 50s in an envelope, be natural with your next customer").

On several occasions Mark visited the bank branches on various days of the week and decided on a Friday, at 12 P.M., as the best time for his attempt. On one occasion he actually went through the motions of an actual heist; waiting in line for the next teller and handing her a one hundred dollar bill, simulating the threatening note, in exchange for five twenties. In effect 'casing the joint'.

Keeping any of the loot was never considered. The challenge was his priority. He selected the target, the Conway Street branch, some six miles from the latest heist. With cash in hand, he would race steadily but quickly from the premises, get lost in the shopping center's noonday crowd, eventually reach his parked car some four blocks away, drive to the midway branch, leave the packet of cash in the deposit slip tray and hopefully not arouse suspicion.

Above it all, his greatest concern was the certainty that all personnel at The County Savings Bank branches were on the alert for any future heists, and of course, the possibility of his failure and potential imprisonment.

The Friday he selected was waiting for him. He studied his list of strategies, typed the threat note, clothed himself with a variety of distracting colors and mentally went through his planned scheme.

"It's now or never," he thought as he drove to a construction sight far from a residential area and parked close by.

Mark walked the four blocks to his target, going through the motions again and again and finally reached his goal. He circled the block several times to dispel the fear that was beginning to unnerve him.

"Maybe this isn't so easy."

With more than a degree of trepidation, Mark entered the bank. He examined the environment and quickly retreated, circled the block once again, and with a final determination, reentered and quickly stood in line with the other customers. Three of them preceded him before he was called, but the call came quickly.

"Sir! You're next! This window!"

Mark walked at a normal pace but unsteadily. The note, small in size, was secreted in his palm. He slid it, face down, through the window slot. The teller, a middle-aged female, froze for the moment but quickly regained her composure although her hands trembled as she quickly placed three packages of fifties in an envelope, pushed it towards Mark who grabbed the envelope and skirted towards the exit. He impulsively turned around noticing that the teller, still aware of the note's threat, had followed his instructions and actually took on the next in line. His breath came in spurts as he walked swiftly through the anticipated noonday crowd, hopefully not provoking a reaction, but once out of range, sprinted the four blocks to his parked car. With tires screeching, he sped the six miles to the next item in his modus operandi: return the cash to the midway branch.

On his arrival, news had already infiltrated the County Savings Bank system that the Conway Street branch had been robbed. Taking advantage of the moment and with a pounding heart, he ambled towards the table holding the deposit and withdrawal slips pretending to select one, hoping that it would appear as an act occurring on a daily basis. Mark joined the customers and bank personnel in their reactions to the news and after noting that no eyes were coming his way, casually placed the envelope in the deposit slip tray and swiftly departed.

On the drive home, despite returning the cash, Mark was beginning to feel the guilt that was not present during all of the hours of preparation or during the actual robbery. On arrival he used the remote to open the garage door but did not enter. Suddenly everything seemed unreal.

He couldn't believe or didn't want to believe that of all the world's population, he alone was the one who robbed the County Savings Bank.

"Did I actually rob a bank? What do I do now? What if the teller remembers me? I really didn't rob the bank! I returned the money! Yeah, they can't do anything to me! I returned the money!" Nonetheless, there it was: a new bold headline on the next day's delivery of 'The Citizen': 'Seventh Heist!'.

Mark's days over the next several months did not allay those concerns but because no federal authorities appeared to be on his trail, they were beginning to dwindle and soon he was conducting himself with an assurance that was there but not wholly up to par.

But that was not to be.

Hamburgers and fries was a meal Mark couldn't resist and constantly found himself in his favorite corner booth indulging at the local fast food diner. On this day two gentlemen in business attire accompanied by a middle-aged female arrived at the scene. The female sat down facing Mark.

"Hey! What's going on here! Get your own seat. And who are you guys?"

"My name is Ann Bailey. I'm the teller at the County Savings Bank. Remember?"

Mark sank in his seat. "And these two men are from the FBI. I was brought here to identify you."

Needless to say, the gig was up. Seven to ten years in a cell that could have been more, but leniency was a consideration for his returning the money.

Released from the upstate federal prison after serving his full term and a more mature twenty-nine year old, Mark was back at his old haunts and with family and friends.

Before entering the County Savings bank, Mark circled the block. He waited in line with the other customers. Three of them preceded him before he was called, but the call came quickly.

"Sir! You're next! This window!"

Mark walked at a normal pace. The note, small in size, was secreted in his palm. He slid it, face down, through the window slot. Ann Bailey read the note, smiled and wished him luck. Mark returned the smile.

The note read, "I swear. Never again!"

THE 'G' CLUB

❖ ❖ ❖ ❖ ❖ ❖ ❖ ❖ ❖ ❖ ❖

There we were, the first generation offspring from the great European influx of the late nineteenth and early twentieth centuries.

America, the promised land, was ours!

Each ethnic group, for security reasons and for language comfort, settled into specific areas. Our domain was comprised primarily of Jews and Italians, followed by those of Irish, Germans, Poles and others in succession.

No, the streets were not paved in gold.

But the benefits were there to be had. A bonding friendship developed, over time, between the eleven and twelve year old Jews and Italians in our area. There were eight of us indulging in sports and other enjoyable pursuits. At times it was necessary, walking to school in twos or threes, to counter any bullying from the German kids from block two or the Irish from block three. No real threats; just a little shoving and pushing as youngsters usually do, but incidents of this kind, grouping in twos or threes to retaliate, strengthened the bonding.

What also held us together too, was the remarkable fact that all eight family names began with the initial 'G': Giordano, Gutfriend, Gordon, Graber, Giuliani, Goodman, Giacometti and Ginsberg. What better incentive was there to have a neighborhood club, a club with a name like The 'G' club.

On occasion, usually on Friday night, we would gather for a club meeting in a friend's kitchen or living room for no reason other than to be together and have a few laughs. Fingertip American cheese sandwiches or other delights almost always awaited us, attesting to that mother's gratification with having her son as part of this friendly group.

By seventeen or eighteen years old, with our 'G' club still enduring, we were heeding the news media's coverage of the rumblings of war in Europe. Not long after, on a Sunday night, came the explosive news delivered without warning: 'Pearl Harbor attacked!' with President Roosevelt's 'day of infamy' speech the following day.

At a hastened club meeting we discussed the possibility of volunteering for service. For most of us, with only our first year of college completed, it would not be easy, but as Americans, volunteering was imperative.

By the first weeks of January, 1942, all had discussed their decisions with family members. From that period till the end of hostilities in September, 1945, no member of the 'G' club had been in contact with another.

With basic training completed, all were immediately deployed to various battle areas. Months and then years passed where 'G' club members were involved in fierce confrontation with the enemy, resulting in most of the members receiving wounds.

As near as remembered...

Anthony Giordano: S/Sgt Army 18th Infantry Division
    Invasion of Europe Wounded
Joseph Gufriend: Capt Army Air Corps
    B-24 Bomber pilot China Prisoner of War
Sidney Gordon: Sgt Army 16th Infantry Division
    Aleutian Islands Wounded
Larry Graber: S/Sgt Army Air Corps C47 Crew
    China Burma India No Wounds
Sal Giuliani: Corporal Marine Corps 6th Marine

Division Solomon Islands Wounded

Martin Goodman: Corporal Marine Corps 12th Marine Division
   Okinawa Wounded

Carl Giacometti: Chief Petty Officer U.S. Navy South
   Pacific Naval Battles No Wounds

Seymore Ginsberg: Sgt Army 14th Infanty Division
   Okinawa Wounded

After enormous loss of life on all sides of the conflict, the battles finally ended; the enemy folded. Unconditional surrender was achieved.

Hugs, kisses and handshakes were administered as each veteran returned home, with some taking longer times than others. Anthony Giordano was detained at the Walter Reed National Military Medical Center in Washington to care for his severe wounds, but eventually all were finally home.

A record of military service was placed in the club files to be available for viewing by future generations, of the rank and achievements of 'G' club members. The exploits of all allied military personnel, ridding the world of the aggressors, gave rise to the expression, 'The Greatest Generation'.

The first priority of the returnees was to reacquaint each with his family and savor the moment when once again our club will meet in some living room or kitchen, devouring those american cheese tidbits.

Appreciative neighbors arranged for a 'G' club gala to welcome home our Jewish and Italian veterans and to thank them for their sacrifice and for the blessing of having all members of the 'G' club able to regain their normal lives.

Now it was time to return to our studies at the various colleges and universities by way of the Veterans' Bill of Rights. Having experienced those lean days of the Great Depression, goals for success were set, and after many semesters and finally into our selected fields and leading up to our thirtieth years, success was achieved:

Anthony Giordano: Owner of engineering firm

Joseph Gutfriend: Neurology surgeon
Sidney Gordon: CEO of electronics firm
Larry Graber: Design director of publishing firm
Sal Giuliani: Clothing manufacturer
Martin Goodman: Importer of fine furniture
Sal Giacometti: Cadillac dealership
Seymour Ginsberg: Attorney for title insurance fund

At age forty it was no longer practical for the 'G' club members to meet on Friday nights or for that matter on any nights. Other priorities of business and family had to be met. Nevertheless, over time, correspondence was there to hold us together as the 'G' club.

On two occasions, during the next fifty years, there was a rebirth of the 'G' club in our old Jewish and Italian neighborhood, a testament to the comradeship of the original.

But peace during that period was not to be. In 1950 a Korean conflict reared it's ugly head. By 1959, another bomb was dropped: Viet Nam, the war that rubbed Americans the wrong way. In both instances the 'G' clubs were disbanded when members were called to duty but were resurrected at wars' end albeit with fewer members, the result of casualties from those tragic engagements.

Some day, with the very first 'G' club membership dwindled down to three or four ninety year olds waiting to join our lifelong friends for another meeting beyond the horizon, our greatest concern would be whether or not the guy upstairs would be serving those luscious, tasty, american cheese tidbits.

PARALLELS

❖❖ ❖❖ ❖ ❖❖ ❖ ❖❖ ❖

His mind absorbed with the events of a long, difficult business day, Lou walked into the late evening gentle rain. From out of nowhere! A volcanic explosion of blinding headlights! Lou shielded his eyes. Too late! The speeding black sedan spin-whipped on the slick surface, its rear fender slamming Lou with a horrifying 'thud', flinging him against a concrete abutment. Regaining control without stopping, the demon accelerated and with tires screeching, disappeared into the avenue's darkness. The gentle rain, unabated, fell on Lou's shattered form.

What seemed a lifetime of a medical team rebuilding his broken body, Lou hoped that by now he would be free of the metal contraption and cast that held his arm in a rigid 'L' position; the upper arm parallel to the ground, the lower arm and hand pointing skyward.

"Get back to your job, your old routine," his doctor advised. "It'll be good for you."

"With this ridiculous contraption?"

"Sure. You think you're the only one who's ever worn one of these things?"

A few days later, having gathered himself mentally to cope with the reaction his 'L' positioned arm might bring, Lou was at his desk answering selected old phone messages and handling accumulated mail. As the noon hour neared, a growling stomach told him it was time for a refill. Walking towards his lunchtime haunt, Lou's eyes caught a vertical cast looming above the crowd. Before he could change his path to avoid an embarrassing confrontation, Lou noted that the owner of the cast had his head tilted to the right; a slight hop in his gait.

"Hey, that's Lester Gordon's funny walk. I'd know that walk anywhere. That has to be Lester. I can't believe it!"

Lou waited till Lester was almost upon him. "Lester Gordon, how the heck are you?"

"Sorry bud, I'm in a hurry." Lester rushed past, awkwardly eyeing Lou's appliance. Then doubling back, "Say, how do you know my name?"

"Lou Giordano from the Bay Streets in Brooklyn," he introduced himself smiling and looking directly into Lester's eyes; intentionally avoiding an examination of his metal brace.

"Lou Giordano? You're kidding! God, I'd never recognize you. It has to be at least thirty years." "Closer to forty," corrected Lou as they grasped each other's free hand. After a few seconds of commiserating expressions, Lou asked. "What the heck happened to you?" "Some son-of-a-bitch, hit-and-run low-life came out of nowhere and shot me about thirty feet onto a concrete sidewalk. If I ever find that guy I'll…"

"Say, hold on. Want to hear something?"

"I won't believe it if you tell me that's what happened to you. I mean that. I won't believe it."

"So don't believe it. But believe *me,* that's why I'm wearing this lousy gadget."

Not withstanding the mutual sympathy, Lou and Lester were exhilarated by this chance meeting. Their minds soon occupied by small talk, neither was aware that the crowd had opened a circular area creating a 'stage' to gawk at this very rare spectacle: Lou's left arm contraption and Lester's right arm contraption formed an amusing mirror image.

Finally onto the staring, the pointing, the aping, Lester asked, "Am I interrupting anything you had planned to do?"

"No. I was just getting something to eat."

"Mind if I join You?"

"I'd like that," answered Lou, thinking how incredible it was that he actually was in the presence of Lester Gordon after all of those years.

"Where do you usually have your lunch Lou?"

"Well, there's a nice coffee house on the next block."

"I think I know the one. Let's go," said Lester, seething as he stared at a young man mimicking the rigid arm position and strutting in a circle to the delight of the onlookers. "Let's get out of here."

Conversation on the short walk unfolded some interesting similarities. Lester and Lou were of the same age, each had two children, one son and one daughter and they were married in the same year, 1960, and speaking of old times after seating themselves, both were startled upon learning their wives came from the same neighborhood and went to the same elementary school.

Interest continued to gather as they realized that both experienced far beyond just a few parallel happenings. They threw names, events and statistics at each other to determine if indeed they lived extraordinarily similar lives. The results were stunning.

"Lou, how old are your children?"

"I have a son twenty-eight and a daughter twenty-five."

"And I have a daughter twenty-eight and a son twenty-five. I swear it."

"I believe you," responded an astonished Lou. "I rely do. But its just so incredible."

"Both married?" asked Lester.

"Both married."

"Grandchildren?"

"Two."

"Me too."

"Ever have any teeth extracted?"

"What do extractions have to do with family?"

31

"Nothing at all. This is getting so mind boggling. I figured a bit of humor might be a relief. No harm done. Right?" A large grin showed that Lester had agreed.

"Let's order some food before we continue," suggested Lester. Lou beckoned to the waiter who flipped to a clean page of his order pad. "I'll have a lettuce and tomato salad with some cottage cheese, light toast, no butter and black coffee."

"I don't believe this," smiled Lester as he duplicated the order. "That's my health-freak lunch. I have it almost every day."

Several times Lou and Lester rested their utensils to focus on a particularly startling revelation. During one of those periods, Lester's concentration was interrupted by George's presence in the coffee shop. "Hey! I know that guy who just came in. George! Over here!" bellowed Lester.

"Really? I know him too," added Lou. "George sells me office supplies."

"He sells them to me too. Sit down and join us George. We've finished but we'll stay with you for a while."

George, rudely not acknowledging the greeting, pulled a chair under him and eyed both casts with a what-happened-to-you-guys expression.

"You won't believe this George. Lou and I met today for the first time in almost forty years and lots of things that have happened to me also happened to him."

"Obviously," injected George.

Lester continued. "Listen to this, George. It's really remarkable. We both got these casts from hit-run drivers, we're both the same age, each of us has a son and a daughter, our wives…"

"So what's the big deal? You're both the same age and have a son and a daughter and both were hit at the same time," responded George.

"No. not at the same time."

"Then it's a *different* accident. So what's he big deal?"

"What I'm trying to tell you is that it was the same *kind* of an accid…"

"OK! OK! Lester. I got the picture. You both were in the same kind of an accident. Big deal." George raised himself from his seat, removed his suit jacket and settled it neatly over the chair back. His stolid expression indicated not the least bit of interest. "What did you guys order?" Lester told him.

"I'll have the same."

"Let's get out of here Lester," said an exasperated Lou.

"No...wait. I want George to hear some of this; as a witness. No one will ever believe what's happening here. Let me see... Okay...Now listen to this George...Lou, were you in World War II?"

"Yes."

"When did you get drafted?"

"I volunteered."

"So did I," added Lester. "When did you volunteer?"

"June one, 1942."

"June two, 1942 for me."

"That's pretty close."

"But different. I feel relieved about that one. Did you get overseas?"

"Yes."

"Where?"

"Burma."

"You're kidding. You were stationed in Burma too? Hey, this is getting ridiculous. If you tell me you were wounded, I'm leaving now."

"Yeah, I got one in the butt."

"I give up. Right or left cheek?"

"Impossible."

"Want to see the evidence?" asked Lou pretending to undo his trouser belt.

George winced. "Nobody wants to see your butt, especially at a lunch table. Some other time Lou, Please."

Where's the waiter? George asked, craning his neck. "I need more coffee. I think both of you guys are nuts."

"Were you in the service George?" inquired Lou sarcastically.

"Of course."

"Overseas?"

"Yes."

"Where?"

"Yangon."

"That's in Burma too!"

"Really?" reacted a surprised George. "I never knew that."

"Well, George, join the group; the guys you call 'nuts'."

Lou and Lester left George with his refilled coffee mug and walked into the still-buzzing lunch crowd. Once again aware of the passersby eyeing their casts, they retaliated by looking squarely back, each with a bent-forward challenging stance.

"Let's get to the corner of the block and talk for a few more minutes," suggested Lou. 'Something's going on here that I just can't let go of. By the way, do you do any traveling?"

"Yes. Matter of fact I was in Italy last Spring."

"Get to Venice?"

"How could anyone go to Italy and not see Venice?"

"I knew it! I knew it! That *was* you in a water bus on the Grand Canal. I was in a gondola with my wife and I told her someone on the bus looked familiar. It was you! I'm sure now. How do you like that?"

"You're probably right. My wife was afraid to get into a gondola. You know we plan to go back again next year."

"When?"

"I'll let you know when we get back."

"No need to tell me anyway. If I decide to go I'm sure we'll meet there."

Lou, after a long pause of both searching their minds for possible areas of similarity, "Let's try a wild one. If you live on Long Island and your town starts with a 'W', just say 'yes'."

"Yes."

"I'm not going to expand on that one, pal," Lou chuckled. "You may be my next door neighbor."

After some smiles, "Say, do you remember the make-up softball games we had every Sunday morning?"

"Sure." recalled Lou. "At Gravesend Park. They were great. And you and I got at least one homer per game. We were known as the 'Homerun Twins'... Right?"

"Yeah, that's right, the 'Homerun Twins'. Gee, that was a long time ago," reminisced Lester.

"Do you think all of this sameness could have started way back then?"

"Could be."

While Lou was thinking back about the fun days on the softball field, Lester threw one at him. "How about your mother's name?"

"Paula." Lou answered quickly.

"Aha! Finally! Not the same!"

"What was your Mother's name?"

"Pauline."

"And that's not coincidental?"

"But it's different. Isn't it?"

"Not really. The derivation is the same."

Lou and Lester dodged the traffic to get back to the street were they first met.

"I'm sure you'll agree that this has been one hell of a day," said Lester as he extended his hand. "Let's go Lou. It's getting late. I'm sure you have to get back to your office. By the way, what do you do for a living?"

"I'm an electrical engineer. And You?"

"A construction engineer."

"This could go on forever."

"Where's your office?"

"Sixtieth and Madison. Six twenty-five."

"Come on. I'll walk you there."

"You're kidding."

"No, I'm not. I've been using those revolving doors for ten years."

Lou thought Lester *was* kidding but found himself in the same elevator. As Lester exited on the tenth floor, Lou pressed his back against the elevator wall. "I'm afraid to ask your shoe size," getting some quizzical looks from the staring passengers. "Twelve C," a smiling Lester shouted back across his cast as the elevator doors closed. Lou, with a much smaller size chortled, "I'll get him on that one next time…for sure."

Lou and Lester took great satisfaction in their newly redeveloped friendship with those never-ending parallel experiences continuing, even to the point of both retiring on the same day. "A controlled parallel," Lou called it.

Lester selected central Florida to spend his remaining days. Lou decided to remain in the northeast, his preference for the variety of seasons being a primary consideration. Reluctantly they parted promising to visit each other at frequent intervals.

The seasons passed and Lou, returning from a golf outing at his country club, entered his foyer as the phone rang. He leaned the club bag against the telephone table.

"Lou? This is Elliot, Lester's brother-in-law. I've got some bad news." After an irritating pause, "So tell me already!"

"OK! OK! Lester was killed in a plane crash a few hours ago. Debbie asked me to call and tell you."

"Oh my god. I can't believe it.'

"The club pro asked Lester to join him for a round on a new golf course," continued Elliot. "Just a short hop on the country club's single prop. I understand the plane's engine conked out over the club house and crashed in a sand trap about a hundred yards from the first tee. Too bad. He was just getting on to the game. Anyway, Debbie asked that I call you. She would like you to attend the service. How about it?"

"Sure. I'll be there. By myself. Susan is taking care of our grandchildren. Their parents are on vacation. Tell Debbie I'll take the first plane in the morning."

A distraught Lou, the phone cradled in his lap, relived their parallel lives but immediately discarded the possibility of a similar, impending violent death.

Dampened by a gentle rain, Lou walked through the boarding gate experiencing more than his usual trepidation. He settled in a 'safe' window seat and quickly secured himself with the seatbelt. His apprehension grew as the plane's acceleration seemed far too great. The ground beneath his window flew past, blurring the concrete runway to a sheet of glass.

"Too fast!" he thought. "We're going too fast!"

The cabin's vibration continued to build as the plane lifted, bringing expressions of muttered anxiety by the passengers. Lou pressed his shoulders against the seat back, his fists tight around the arm rests, his heart pounding.

Leveling at 35,000 feet, the plane rolled uneasily to the left. Lou's eyed were the first to catch the engine's belching smoke; then... a violent burst of flame, triggering an explosive force tearing the wing from the fuselage.

Lou and Lester were eulogized simultaneously and placed in the ground parallel to each other. The chiseled names on their stones would bear the same initials.

"You died your violent death June one. Is that right?" asked Lou.

"Right," confirmed Lester. "And You?"

"I died my violent death June two."

"That's pretty close, Lou, pretty close," chuckled Lester. "But different."

AN AMERICAN JOURNEY

❖ ❖

It was 8:30 in the evening, September 15th, in the year 1902, in Rzerschev, a small town just northeast of Vienna, in Austria. Huddling around the lantern on the kitchen table were members of the family, planning for their venture in the new world. A decision was made. One member of the family was to travel to America, specifically to the city of New York and its lower east side. The purpose was clear. They had to improve their lives, their fortunes.

Eighteen year old Wolf, the youngest of the five siblings, convinced his parents that while all members were contributing to the family stability, however meager, he alone was the most expendable.

Why the lower east side of New York City? Correspondence from those who relocated, to families remaining in Rzerschev, almost always mentioned the comfort, the vitality of their new environment. Wolf's objective was to determine if this was actually so, the ideal place for his family to lay the foundation for a new life.

Pooling their resources allowed Wolf to board a train to Rottedam, Holland, where he embarked on the steamer Columbia. Twelve days later, after a choppy voyage and tolerating the vigorous procedures of Ellis Island, he arranged for a sparse but adequate space in a rooming house; a rooming house on New York's lower east side.

His first thoughts as he merged into the throngs on Hester Street, his new address, were not particularly encouraging. Yes throngs! It seemed that every square inch was occupied by humanity, pushcart entrepreneurs selling their wares from kitchen items to articles of clothing, fruit and vegetables were for sale on horse drawn wagons, children darting here and there with no apparent parental guidance, animated groups congregating every so often discussing whatever; all best described as controlled chaos. Yet there was one redeeming feature: Yiddish was the common language; Wolf's language.

After some weeks of digesting the general climate of life in this slice of America and despite his initial impression he had of his Hester Street neighborhood and gaining insight from those who arrived previously from eastern Europe, Wolf felt his elderly parents would be comfortable in this atmosphere, this promised land, with people of their own kind.

Settling himself one evening in his modest surroundings, he decided that prior to his elderly parents starting a new life, it was imperative that he have even a modest income for them and himself, albeit in a position above that of pushcart entrepreneur.

Over time, Wolf met, introduced and was introduced to those firmly established in this bustling east side, taking advantage of those who had developed business associations. Someone suggested that he contact a Mr. Solomon, a manufacturer of women's coats and suits situated on 37th Street between Sixth and Seventh Avenue. Perhaps there was an opening. Amazingly, with no resume and no experience in the field and only good fortune, Wolf was hired! After some basic instructions, he was responsible for unrolling heavy bolts of cloth over long production tables where patterns for the clothing were outlined prior to being cut. Adding to his good fortune, Solomon spoke Yiddish and also English to those beyond his midtown business address.

After many months on the job, Wolf, surprisingly, was able to suggest improvements with respect to production. Solomon was impressed and recognized the potential in this energetic, devoted employee and rewarded him, over a period, with major manufacturing responsibilities, generally relegated to those with much more experience, resulting in considerable increases in Wolf's income.

Improbable as it may seem, in a relatively short time, Wolf accumulated sizable savings allowing him to improve his life style and to consider an appropriate time to bring his parents to the hustle and bustle of New York's east side.

With his help and close relatives in Rzerschev, Wolf's parents were able to be greeted by Lady Liberty. A two bedroom furnished rental apartment, minutes from Hester Street, was leased by Wolf for himself and the newly arrived Golda and Michael, both of whom were overjoyed with the prospects of a new, more comfortable existence; an existence well beyond its presence in Rzerschev.

Looking down the road, Wolf's mind centered on his recently acquired dream: a successful clothing manufacturing firm. With many problems involved in putting together a complicated business of this kind and despite the quirks of competition, an additional major concern remained. Since only a few English expressions infiltrated Wolf's Yiddish, English speaking sales personnel were required on staff if he were to successfully sell his designer clothing to upscale department stores and boutiques.

It was several seasons after Solomon's retirement that Wolf had his new midtown establishment on solid ground and gaining large orders of his stylish garments.

Unselfishly, Wolf used his own funds for his older brothers, Max and Ben, to make the crossing and arranged for their temporary living quarters; his other siblings deciding to remain in their accustomed Rzerschev.

To help with the adjustment in their new surroundings, Wolf employed Max with the very same responsibility given him by Solomon: unrolling those heavy bolts of cloth over long production tables. Ben tied the cut sections of cloth with discarded strips for safe keeping. Their immediate response on that first day at the table was that what their young brother had accomplished was incredulous; the many he employed, the immense area needed for production, the vast inventory of cloth, the exquisite final products, the professional models parading before the buyers from those high end department stores; truly an aura of success.

Also, beyond belief, he had a secretary!

Adding to his extraordinary good fortune, Wolf, a handsome well-built man of neat attire, immediately impressed a beautiful young lady at a Seder dinner where both were asked to attend. Before the year had ended, true romance entered the scene and soon after marriage arrangements were addressed to the delight and approval of both proud parents.

As the seasons passed, thanks to his business acumen and prestigious style awards presented at the esteemed yearly New York fashion shows, Wolf was able to purchase a magnificent home in Bensonhurst, a well-to-do section of Brooklyn where he and his wife, Jenny, their two children, Irving, age five and Pearl, nearing her second birthday, along with Golda and Michael, settled in comfortably.

From out of nowhere, the new fullness of Wolf's life was interrupted by an abrupt decline in the purchasing power of the 'good faith' dollar; the stockmarket had crashed! The Great Depression was upon us. Wolf's successes, his business, his home, his lifestyle in jeopardy, he still had sufficient savings to sustain his family and those of his brothers, Max and Ben, who were also experiencing difficulties during this trying period. Without their asking, he volunteered to assist with the cost of rent, the monthly food tabs at Meyer's butcher shop and Hyman's grocery. Also incidental medical and dental fees at a time when the word 'copay' was not yet introduced in our dictionaries.

Despite all the suffering, the food lines, the non-existent employment, the U.S., this great democracy, eventually prevailed.

Behind the scene, these many years past, since settling in Hester Street was his determination to speak English with a non-descernable accent on a level with that of a bright high school student. To this end he hired a elementary school teacher to provide the heavy artillery in his quest. Success was to be a foregone conclusion. And so it was. Besides gaining citizenship in this great country of America, speaking English fluently was indeed, icing on the cake.

Adding to his life of accomplishment, Wolf was proud of his ability to provide the means for his childrens' educations and particularly so, when they were awarded college degrees, some with doctorates, contrary to the unavailable higher education facilities in the year 1902, in Rzerschev.

It was 8:30 in the evening, September 15th, in the year 1954, when members of the family were huddled not around a lantern on the kitchen table in Rzerschev, but under an elegant dining room chandelier in upper New York City, celebrating the seventieth birthday and American journey of Wolf, my father, my hero, my friend.

THE BET

❖ ❖ ❖ ❖ ❖ ❖ ❖

"You're nuts Sal…really nuts." Benny slapped the air inches from Sal's face. "Are you telling me a war hero is buried in our church graveyard? C'mon. No Revolutionary War battles were fought within three hundred mlles of here, right? And besides, most of us take the cemetery short cut to get to school. Any of you other people ever see the grave?" Nobody did. "You're nuts Sal…really nuts."

Only slightly ruffled by Benny's evaluation of his mental faculty, Sal calmly swung one of his western boots onto the desktop, getting himself more comfortable on the hardwood seat. He folded his dark glasses over the v-neck of his sweater and continued in an easy manner. "Look, my dad is a history buff and really into the Revolution and almost felt he participated and because of that he developed a sort of…you know…a kinship, yeah a kinship…with the hero buried across the road. He used to take me there when I was a kid."

Benny pretended not to be listening. His eyes were tracing the baroque plaster designs on the classroom ceiling, his fingers drumming his knees. With only a small hint of annoyance at Benny's antics, Sal walked slowly to the large series of windows and gazed out. He reached for his glasses as his eyes locked onto a small corner of the churchyard that extended from behind the church.

"Just a minute…let me think," his fingers brushing his brow. "I can't remember the guy's name on the stone but beneath it, it reads 'Revolutionary War Hero' then…I think…'Born 1756… Died 1779' Yeah, that's it!" Sal turned from the window and looked squarely at Benny, his arms folded across his chest with an air of assurance. "Believe me Benny, it's there."

Benny slapped the air once again. He bent forward, stiffened his arms against the sill of the window and stared up at the expanse of blue sky. Seconds later, his eyes caught the same small corner of the graveyard.

"There's no hero's grave there," he stated with authority and then, with a fiery voice and thrusting his finger at Sal to underscore each word. "I know everything about this town. I've lived here all my life!"

"We can settle this all in a few minutes by going across the road," advised Gary, Sal's varsity team buddy. Benny's jaw was set. "Nothing's going to be there Gary. I know that graveyard."

"Okay, smart guy, how about this," spurted a by now exasperated Sal. "You get twenty dollars from me if it's not there, you sleep on the grave all night, tonight, if it is…Okay?"

"That's stupid. Why do we have to do anything like that. Let's just go and see if it's there."

A smirk replaced the impatience in Sal's expression. "Backing out already…"

"Okay! Okay!" Benny steamed. That's no big deal. The bet's on. Let's go to the graveyard."

The stone was there. A rather small marker, easily hidden in the midst of much taller ones.

"There he is! See?" pointed Sal. "Yeah and that's his name, 'James Filmore Henry'. Not an easy one to remember. And it says he's a 'Revolutionary War Hero'. See Benny?…Right there."

Benny was taken back. He squinted his eyes, not really wanting to see the stone in full light. "I've been through this graveyard a thousand times…Damn…I'll probably have to sleep here tonight. For sure these guys won't let me out of it."

A few paces from the handful of curious classmates examining the historic marker, Sal was in a hand-over-mouth conversation with Gary, Benny eyeing them furtively. As the group neared the wrought iron gate leading to the outside pavement, Sal confirmed Benny's foreboding. "Gary and I will pick you up at 9:00 tonight. Okay Benny? And we'll drive back here."

"Damn, They're really going to do it."

"Why are we driving? We can walk here."

"Never mind. We're just picking you up. You'll see why later."

At precisely 9:00 o'clock, Sal's car raced in, tires screeching to a halt. Benny stood up from the wooden steps of his front porch and slowly approached the car; trepidation in his eyes. "Sure you want to go through with this?" he asked. Sal's unrelated response, "Hop in. Let's get going," irritated Benny.

"Where's Gary?"

"He'll meet us there."

Gary was leaning against the wrought iron gate, his bent knee braced against a fence spike. A considerable length of clothesline was looped around his shoulder.

"What the hell is the rope for?"

"You'll see Benny."

The three walked in, single file, to the gravesight with no conversation until… "Okay, let's get to it. Let's have the line," Sal commanded. "Raise your arms so I can get around your waist."

"Hey, hold on a minute. What are you guys doing?"

"That's to make sure you stay put," Gary's answer coming before Benny completed his question.

The rope was double-knotted near the small of Benny's back. Two long ends remained beyond the knot.

"Down you go Benny."

Benny laid himself gingerly on the gave, his head inches from the headstone, cold shivers twitching his flesh. Sal wrapped one of the ends securely around the stone and used a double knot again. Benny complained, "Jesus".

"Like I said, we're just making sure you don't leave before morning," a nearly sadistic smile working Gary's face.

Sal gathered both ends and handed them to Gary who walked down an aisle some twenty-five feet to the wrought iron fence. Benny was incensed by his classmates' obviously prearranged strategy as the lines were tossed through the fence between two spikes. Gary collected them and bound them to the steering post of his Chevy parked at the curb, slamming the door shut, allowing only minimal slack back to Benny.

A twinge of guilt found its way into Gary's chest. With his eyes gazing at, but not really seeing the ground, he ambled back to the gravesight trying to console himself with some offhand reasoning. "A bets a bet," he mumbled.

Sal and Gary checked the rope attachments one last time before departing. Satisfied that Benny was securely bound, Sal attempted to lighten the tension with some humor but it was clumsy, insensitive. "You know Benny, lying there you look like a dead ringer for the hero."

"Yeah, and we'll come by tomorrow morgue...ing to pick you up," added Gary.

Benny was amused by it all but his smile didn't come easily. It was a nervous smile, tight against his cheeks.

"Good night friends," Benny delivered sarcastically as the two walked towards the gate, looking back occasionally at the sight of Benny lying on the hero's gave. Sal gave a choppy goodbye wave as they reached the sidewalk pavement.

He was alone now, suddenly aware of the eerie quiet. The air was crisp, chilling to the marrow. Light from the moon engulfed the graveyard like a stage setting, etching deep black shadows, attracting the eye to every detail. The almost-daylight was great enough for Benny to read the chiseled names on headstones several yards from where he was lying. His teeth bit the inside of his cheek as he was drawn to the excess earth piled on a nearby grave. At the foot of the pile a propped marker named the recently deceased. It reminded Benny of the small card used to identify a row of vegetables in his backyard garden. Overgrown grass and weeds of the unattended grounds cascaded over the names of the smaller stones, some of which lost the caring of relatives and friends. Other stones appeared to have fallen prey to the elements, losing the grip of the surrounding earth. They were lying face up, joining the permanent occupants in death.

Engine shut...lights out, Gary's chevy glided noiselessly to within thirty yards of where Benny was lying. From the darkened interior they could view the lower part of Benny's form, assuring his presence. Benny had no idea they had returned; the hero's stone blocking his view.

For all his tribulation, he was determined not to make any effort to leave. "After all," he reflected, "it's only one night of my life. Tomorrow we'll probably have a big laugh about this."

After a few hours of getting accustomed to his dilemma, "I wonder what the hero below me was like. Is he really all bones down there? What made him a hero...and at such a young age?" Benny was beginning to develop a kinship with the hero much as Sal's father did. "Hey you down there! Bet you're wondering why I'm lying on your grave."

Benny, playing games, waited some seconds for the hero's response then smiled to himself. "And I thought Sal was nutty."

The unsettling quite, still with him, was broken by a meandering cat whose paws snapped an occasional dry leaf in its path. It stopped and stared statue-like at Benny, it's eyes reflecting the intensity of the moonlight. Seconds later, unsure of its surroundings, it snarled and darted into the darkness. For the moment, despite his being unnerved, anything moving was a relief for Benny.

He looked at his watch...4:00 A.M. Not too long before daylight. The cold air was beginning to numb him. Using the palm of his hand, he massaged the length of his left arm to generate some warmth. Then...reaching to rub his right arm, something! somebody!...pulled him quickly into the grave. Benny's chest heaved for air...his heart pounding. He arched his back, craning his neck to see who or what it was; the rope slack restricting him. His mind raced. Was it the hero who was grabbing him? Why? For what? With breath shortened, Benny was unable to dislodge the scream gorging his throat.

Benny couldn't know that the hero's rotted pine casket had given way to the earth above, compounded by Benny's weight. The space left by the collapsed box was quickly filled crashing Benny's body into the resulting depression at ground level.

The early morning light awakened Sal and Gary.

"Jesus, I can't believe it. Looks like Benny's asleep," Sal whispered to himself. "How can he fall asleep on a grave. Jesus".

Leaving the car, the two strolled the pavement to the cemetery gate, Gary bellowing, "Hey, Benny, time to get up!" Benny didn't respond. The feeling in their guts immediately signaled that all was not well. Their pace quickened to a trot. Both leaped over the line from the wrought iron fence to the steering post of the parked car. The stone that shielded their position several hours before did not allow them to see Benny's face… not until they were almost upon him…to experience severe shock, utter disbelief.

Benny's face was frozen in a hideous expression; his bulging, inflamed eyes almost cast loose from their sockets, mouth agape, lips pulled back, teeth bared. Sal and Gary could only stare at Benny, …with shame. "What have we done. Jesus… What have we done." After a period of controlled panic, they became aware of, but were unable to determine the reasons for what had occurred. Mysteriously, the ground beneath Benny was lower by at least a measured foot. His arms and legs were outstretched over the lip of the depression. Benny seemed to have used his fingers and the heels of his shoes to claw the earth in a desperate attempt to halt his drop into the grave.

Sal broke Gary's staring spell. "Let's untie him," he snapped, contemplating the eventual arrival of authorities. They found the line around the stone was not easy to undo, and getting to the knot ay Benny's back was also not a simple matter. Turning Benny's dead-weight body in the depression eliminated the line slack from the parked Chevy. Gary ran to the car and untied the line. They lifted Benny by his hands and feet, opened the knot at his back, loosening the loop, and carefully replaced him in the grave.

Gary collected the clothesline, looped it one again around his shoulder and strode to the public phone at the cross street. He dialed 911.

Walking back slowly to the wrought iron gate, Gary once again searching the ground, unable to to quell the shame. He entered the graveyard head down, shoulders drooped, unaware of the crushing scene he was about to encounter. Almost at the gravesight he raised his eyes. Sal was in a crunched-up fetal position lying crosswise on top of Benny, his conscience and physical being destroyed by the excruciating guilt he suffered for Benny's violent death. Before Gary could complete the sign of the cross over his heart, his body convulsed. A massive cardiac explosion tore the inside of his chest. Keeling over with no attempt to break his fall, he was dead before his body draped over Sal and Benny.

"Ever see anything like this?" asked the Chief of Detectives. His deputies, eyes riveted, were not able to respond. Three dead young men, heaped on an already occupied grave, was not an easy scene.

Moonlight etched deep black shadows in the graveyard where Benny, Sal and Gary were interred side by side. The eerie quiet was was broken by a meandering cat, it's paws snapping an occasional dry leaf as it scampered over the three gravesights.

GIACOMO'S GIFT

❖ ❖ ❖ ❖ ❖ ❖ ❖ ❖ ❖ ❖ ❖ ❖ ❖ ❖

There it was, the single word 'urinal' written longhand on a one-by-two inch slip of paper, folded in half...and half again. Giacomo had selected it from a small pile of fifteen slips placed on the large design table by Mr. Arbuthnot who then shuffled the pile with his forefinger, believing this to be the most equitable method of assigning projects for his art class: Industrial Design 1.

A middle-aged Scotsman given occasionally to levity, Mr. Arbuthnot's suspender colors always complemented those of his bow tie, his gold key chain extending from suspender button to pants pocket looped itself to some studio equipment with regularity. Nevertheless, he was revered as the most effective motivator at the Art Institute and insisted on professional standards from all who attended his class.

'Telephone', 'Toaster', 'Iron' and the like, other items to be designed and crafted in Mr. Arbuthnot's shuffled pile, were chosen by more fortunate students. Clearly, designing a urinal was not the most glamorous subject in the selection process.

Giacomo, a young, stern-faced independent with long, slim, artistic fingers belying a muscular Italian frame, regarded his urinal project as a challenge. He was determined to embrace the principles of design practiced by the famous in the world of sculpture. Also, he reflected, someone had to fashion this object simply because of its need and practical use and then there is the sense of gratification knowing that one had created a prototype for the masses.

Completing several preliminary drawings which gained great praise from Mr. Arbuthnot, Giacomo further developed three concepts showing front and side views with rendered shading to simulate the dimensions of the urinal. After a lengthy evaluation, they could not agree on which design to pursue. Mr. Arbuthnot bristled when Giacomo, being his own man, chose the one he felt had the most aesthetic qualities.

Eagerly getting on with the project, he quickly constructed an armature, the wire skeleton that would hold the weight of the malleable clay used to model the final shape. Giacomo began to structure the clay with an enthusiasm he never experienced with any previous creative endeavor.

After several weeks of patiently working every subtle curve and sweeping depression, he began to realize that the masterfully-shaped tools were, in his mind, actual extensions of his fingers. There was nothing separating his creation from himself; it and he were indeed one body. Watering the clay to eliminate any trace of surface imperfection, he stepped back to admire what consumed so many diligent hours. Giacomo was thrilled with the symmetry, the dynamism, the utter perfection of his urinal.

Plaster casting the clay models sculpted in the industrial design class, a delicate procedure, required the expertise of an artisan. The institute had one in always-aproned Louis Pinchot, a full-waisted Parisian with a dockworker's hands and a surgeon's finesse. Despite the privilege of having Mr. Pinchot cast his sculpture with what he was sure would be a precise technique and with artistic attention paid to all the refinements of his finished piece, Giacomo nevertheless insisted on supervising the pouring of the mold, much to the dismay of Mr. Pinchot. As a result, some minor imperfections remained at the seam separating the two pieces of the mold. Moistened, very fine sandpaper not only eliminated the scars but finished the surface with a sheen simulating the glaze of an actual urinal.

During the entire period that the urinal was being fashioned, Norma, introverted, frail to the point of anorexia, faced Giacomo across the studio table. Herself envied at the institute for having an innovative sense of design, she marveled at his artistic approach. Each morning he would arrive well before the other students, don a pale blue smock and quickly involve himself with the project. By the time Norma settled herself at her work area, he was immersed, jockeying back and forth to view his creation from various perspectives; softening a curve, smoothing a recess.

Being a bit skittish and not wanting to chance embarrassment, Norma chose not to ask Giacomo what he had selected from the small pile of folded slips shuffled by Mr. Arbuthnot. The other students admired Giacomo's feeling for design and his technical achievements but never discussed the fact that the finished piece would be a urinal. Consequently, she never knew what he object across the table represented.

At the term's end Giacomo, with the help of his classmates, carried the heavy original clay to the back of a borrowed van and delivered it to his apartment kitchen, partially converted to a studio. The midday light, streaming in, flowed around the urinal; the heavy shadows and highlights accentuating the magnificence of the forms. Exhilarated with the effect of the illumination, Giacomo was once again stirred to working on his creation.

Holding the bottom half of the clay steady with his left arm, and nestling the top half in the crook of his right elbow, he began to slowly rotate both parts in opposite arcs. The immediate effect was startling. What was once a urinal was converted to an elegant human torso bent at the waist culminating in an exquisite curve from hip to shoulder.

Imposing on Mr. Pinchot to cast his new version which he titled 'Torso One', Giacomo had to first agree not to supervise the procedure. After drying and the necessary refinements accomplished, the plaster model was introduced to a local prestigious gallery which placed it in its front window facing the avenue. An immediate success, the sculpture drew raves from influential art critics. Elated with the very favorable reaction, Giacomo, with a Mr. Delaquoix, had the plaster model trucked to a foundry where it was transformed to copper after being enlarged proportionately to a height of twelve feet. Lowered by hoist into a metallic bath, it emerged with a brilliant, sparkling chrome surface. The workers, struck with awe at the sight, broke out with spontaneous applause. Some removed their grimy work gloves and shook Giacomo's hand.

The cost of this expensive operation was incurred by Mr. Delaquoix, an erect, lean, fortyish with aquiline features, impeccably attired and whose constant companion was a polished ebony cane capped with the silver head of a wolfhound. Mr. Delaquoix championed the sculptor after viewing 'Torso One' at the gallery. Not wanting to part with his creation, Giacomo and his backer came to terms: In payment for his patronage, upon Giacomo's death, 'Torso One' was to become the property of Mr. Delaquoix.

Brought to the attention of the principles of the Modern Art Museum by Mr. Delaquoix, 'Torso One' was immediately displayed in a place of honor. Staring in disbelief at the splendor and majesty of this exquisite piece, the Director of Acquisitions offered Giacomo whatever price he asked for 'Torso One' to become part of the museum's permanent collection. Despite the agreement with Mr. Delaquoix forbidding any arrangement with the museum, Giacomo would never have acceded to the director's proposition; he and 'Torso One' were one, an inseparable part of each other.

On occasion, Giacomo yielded, though reluctantly, to the wishes of museums and private collectors who wanted desperately to purchase any of his pieces. Huge amounts of money were offered by them even for uncompleted projects knowing that anything Giacomo Giacometti sculpted would be a masterpiece.

As the years passed, Giacomo's 'Torso One', on exhibition at the major museums and art galleries of the world, added to his soaring reputation. He was honored by all the distinguished art societies and respected by many as possibly the sculptor of he century.

Arranging for a one-man Giacomo Giacometti show at a London gallery, Mr Delaquoix never returned. There were no answers to his whereabouts and findings from official investigations never indicated if any deductions were drawn. He seems to have just faded away. After several years and applying the statute of limitations, Giacomo felt his pact with Mr. Delaquoix was rescinded. "Amen.", he thought, but what will happen to 'Torso One' after I'm gone".

Norma, his colleague from across the design table read in the Giornale D'Italia that Giacomo Giacometti would be hosting the opening of the neo-impressionistic sculpture show where his 'Torso One' was currently on limited loan and the most important piece to be shown. Living for many years with her Italian husband and children in Florence, she had no opportunity until now to visit the very famous Giacomo. Contacting him through the show sponsors, Norma was asked to be his guest at a private viewing which she was sure to regard as one of the highlights of her life.

Despite the years, they recognized each other immediately and embraced. After a champagne toast, Norma and Giacomo walked slowly, arm in arm, to the gallery area reminiscing about Mr. Arbuthnot. Having experienced more of life, her shyness no long a problem, she asked, "Giacomo, please tell me what you were designing so many years ago in our industrial design class."

"You mean my urinal?"

"A urinal?...a urinal? That beautiful shape you created was a urinal? Come off it! What do you think I am!

At that moment, looking beyond Giacomo's shoulder, Norma's eyes locked onto 'Torso One'. Sitting on a black stone base, a strategically placed light source emphasizing every nuance of form, the gleaming chrome sculpture shown with an intoxicating brilliance.

57

"Giacomo…breathtaking, marvelous!"…her body tingling from the effect of this superlative piece. Suddenly gathering herself mentally, Norma bent forward slightly, staring intently at 'Torso One' for many seconds. "You know, your sculpture looks vaguely familiar. Then, "Oh no!…It couldn't be…Giacomo, this isn't…Oh my god, is it?" Giacomo, flexing his still muscular frame, looked straight into Norma's piercing, inquisitive eyes, his lips parting to a faint smile and offered no reply. There was no need. As they slowly departed the gallery area, Norma placed her hand in his, feeling the electricity of Giacomo's genius flow into her being.

Yes, she thought, while the urinal was a prototype for the masses, 'Torso One' was indeed a gift for humanity…Giacomo's gift.

FLYING THE HUMP

In late 1942, WWII, at the age of 19 and a member of the 10th Air Corps, a part of the China, Burma, India Theatre of Operations, I found myself stationed in Chabua, a small village in northern India. A cargo aircraft, a C-47, was awaiting my arrival. I was selected from the new recruits to replace Hank, an experienced crew member, who didn't survive a crash landing in China.

Supplies of fifty gallon drums of high octane fuel, bombs, machine gun ammunition, mortar shells, truck and aircraft engines and hospital equipment had to be delivered by air, non-stop twenty four hours into Kunming, China. Our mission was to enable the Chinese army and the U.S. Army 14th Air Corps to remain effective and keep pressure on Japanese occupational troops.

China's eastern seaports were closed by Japanese invasion troops and the Japanese navy. The only available route to China from India was by air over the Himalaya Mountains, commonly referred to as 'The Hump' where extremely severe weather existed on a daily basis, severe enough to occasionally bring down an aircraft; where a single high caliber bullet from a Japanese fighter out of Burma striking our fuel laden drums would transform our C-47 into an instant fireball.

Not adding to the morale were the living and working conditions which were basically primitive. My crew and I lived in bamboo bashas. During the monsoon season temperatures were extremely hot with very high humidity. The entire base was a sea of mud requiring the airstrips to be constructed with steel mats. There were no hangers for aircraft maintenance which had to be done at night due to the heat. Our clothes and shoes mildewed within days. Meals consisted of C-rations. Malaria and dysentery were prevalent diseases.

Despite these dreadful conditions, success had to be unconditional.

Headquarters worked our schedules requiring us to be ready and able to accomplish our missions. On my fifth flight, a night flight over the Hump, I was still very naive about the vast dangers incurred on almost a daily basis and despite experiencing critical weather patterns and the probability of a Japanese encounter, incredibly, fear was not a factor. For a nineteen year old, this was going to be 'easy as pie.' Until...

"Fire! port engine! Everybody out!" commanded Jeff, our twenty-two year old pilot. Except for me, panic was at a minimum with the rest of the crew.

"I'm not going anywhere!"

"Okay then, stay and die!," someone shouted. The threat threw me immediately back to my senses. I quickly donned my parachute and with a nudge from behind, and a pounding heart, was the second of the crew to throw myself into the vast, open sky.

After a breathtaking free fall, the chute bellowed open. Although recovered somewhat from the nauseating, compelling decision of having to make the jump, I still felt overcome with cold shivers, especially when looking down at the earth from seven or eight thousand feet on this moonless night unable to clearly define any landmarks.

Suddenly, a blinding flash! Our C-47 had disintegrated! It had fallen prey to the high octane fuel in contact with the blazing engine as it plowed into the upper rocky outcroppings of the Hump. The explosive force opened up the night, allowing me to view the ground for some seconds, offering a picture of a rocky surface I was headed for.

I landed with a hard 'thud' and gathered the silk canopy. By daylight, despite scrapes and bruises, the crew was able to gather ourselves and waited for several hours for the search and rescue group of the Air Transport Command who returned us to our base.

At headquarters the crew was asked for details of our experience, a common practice of investigation used to determine causes of unusual death threatening situations.

Two days later I was looking down at the ricepaddies as we approached Kunming with a load of supplies and a string of bullet holes between the engine and the fuselage.

After a gale driven difficult landing, inspection revealed bullets had penetrated the hospital equipment within bare inches of our fuel drums and ammunition. The dreaded fireball had been averted! It was time to acknowledge that this tour of duty was not going to be 'easy as pie '.

I'LL BE SEEING YOU

❖ ❖ ❖ ❖ ❖ ❖ ❖ ❖ ❖ ❖ ❖ ❖ ❖ ❖ ❖ ❖ ❖ ❖

*(Although most would dismiss my assertion that
as young teenagers we had a little boyfriend
or girlfriend, the truth is, we all did.)*

Annette was thirteen, I was fourteen. Summer recess
allowed our group of young friends to congregate daily at a
hangout in our special corner of Gravesend Park. On this day,
I found myself sitting next to Annette. There was something
about her that seemed different today. She was always pretty
in my mind, but today, for whatever reason, she appeared
to be beautiful. Perhaps it was my being closer to her than
ever before. Five of us on a bench, that was designed for four
sitting comfortably, brought our bodies in close contact. Then
something I had not prepared for happened. I slowly slid my
arm around her waist. Annette turned her beautiful face to
mine and after a few seconds, smiled. My arm remained in that
position for the remainder of the afternoon. When it was time
for us to break up, I decided to walk with Annette the several
blocks to her apartment. As we prepared to leave the park, to my
utter gratification, she held my hand and did not let go until we
reached her door. Before entering, she asked that we sit together
whenever we were at the park. I kissed her cheek. She smiled
and entered her apartment. I turned and left for home.

We saw each other frequently in the park and continued our
childhood relationship, always close to each other. Some time

after, her parents divorced. I felt depressed when I learned that Annette's mother decided to be with her unmarried sister in Arizona and Annette was ordered by the court, because of her age, to accompany her. Years later, a mutual friend happened upon Annette. He was introduced to her husband and two young children. When the occasion presented itself, Annette asked about me. Before leaving, my friend was given a photograph of herself and her children along with his promise to send her love.

Annette was just as beautiful as ever.

I'LL BE SEEING YOU

❖❖❖❖❖❖❖❖❖❖❖❖❖❖❖❖❖❖

(Sequel, as young adults.)

Elaine and I met on a blind date with my cousin and his blind date. It was on the Sunday in 1941 when Pearl Harbor was attacked. She was seventeen and I was nineteen. After the usual introductions, and to my extreme pleasure, Elaine placed her arm in mine as we proceeded to a prearranged dinner at an upscale restaurant. Unbelievably, there was something about her beauty and soft spoken approach that caused me to feel that I would love to be with her forever. After some time getting to know each other and discussing our life's dreams and during a period between meal courses, Elaine managed to find my hand and held it on her lap beyond the eyes of my cousin and his date. I didn't know why, but I felt I had to kiss her cheek. On the way to her home, her arm remained in mine. At her door we hugged and promised to date none other. We often went dancing at some social club or some houseparty where the beautiful song 'I'll Be Seeing You' was played. It was our favorite and it soon became the favorite of the boys serving overseas. I volunteered for the Army Air Corps and Elaine promised to wait for me. Six months after I returned we were married. Sixty three years later we were still dancing to our recording of 'I'll Be SeeingYou'.

TURNABOUT

❖ ❖ ❖ ❖ ❖ ❖ ❖ ❖ ❖ ❖

It was 5:45 P.M. on a chilly Autumn evening. Office hours had ended. The elevator was waiting. At each floor the entrant was greeted by the friendship developed by those with similar long periods of employment at the same location. Except for a new arrival, an arrival that entered from the third floor, pushing his way into the tight-knit group, using his elbows to gain more space for himself and whose eyes, at the same time, were focused on the art deco patterns lining the elevator ceiling; obviously an attempt at nonchalance. Blake felt for the small pistol he carried legally. He wanted to be prepared in the event the uninvited stranger's actions became more than merely abusive.

The ride ended. Out poured the employees with their 'Thank God It's Friday' attitudes. The stranger remained behind for some minutes but walked steadily through the empty lobby and through the revolving doors leading to the street. He hurried to join the elevator group and others from the general business area now bunched to beat the chill in the bus shelter at the nearby corner. Blake was not particularly concerned that the stranger in the elevator was now shoulder to shoulder with him in the narrow confines of the shelter.

The crosstown path to Pennsylvania Station was uneventful as usual except for the stranger whose eyes were locked onto Blake standing some five feet from him in the heavily crowded bus. On occasion Blake would intentionally reposition himself and again face the stranger whose stare was constant; becoming more than just an annoyance.

At the stop, Blake scrambled from the bus and headed to the escalator leading down to the station departure area. With a gut feeling he turned to find the stranger on the top step of the escalator at the same moment that he stepped off. Immediately, a decision hit him. He would stop at one of the stalls in the promenade pretending to purchase a drink, compelling the stranger to pass him. To Blake's distress, the stranger lingered until Blake finished his drink, then ambled past him and was eventually lost in the course of the thousands heading home for their weekend respite.

The Babylon train was already fifteen minutes overdue when Blake joined the cluster of disgruntled passengers. He gave little thought of the stranger as he joined those who were voicing their displeasure at the delay. Another fifteen minutes passed before a general sigh of relief was apparent as the lighted display board announced the arrival on the Babylon track.

Blake settled in a window seat and was startled when he caught the stranger walking hurriedly past him and into the following car searching for the few seats remaining. But he soon returned, obviously unsuccessful, and joined other standing passengers. He spread open a late newspaper edition and pretended to scan the pages, occasionally peering at Blake just beyond the top of the open spread.

Then it happened! Quickly folding his newspaper, the stranger pushed his way through the cramped aisle, his eyes not leaving Blake. The passengers loudly mouthed their disapproval as he re-entered the car where he previously searched for a seat. Another overbearing annoyance that Blake could not tolerate.

But the stranger was not finished with his antics. He soon returned and again pushed his way through the crowded aisle to where Blake was sitting, stared at Blake for several seconds and quickly retreated, the irate passengers beginning to pummel him as he made his way back.

That incident coupled with the other aggravating theatrics was too much to bear. "Who the hell is this psycho, his motives. Am I going to let this guy continue to bug me or do I disregard him as a lunatic from some nut house."

But soon, Blake, nonetheless, developed an aversion, a loathing, that was beginning to fester since the aggravating encounter on the bus ride to Pennsylvania Station. He decided that before leaving the train he would physically approach this lowlife. He had had enough of him; perhaps slap him around a bit to express his contempt.

At the Babylon station, Blake, disgruntled, left the car and stopped on the platform searching to see if this screwball had departed or remained on the train. Unfortunately the passengers scurrying in many directions made it difficult for him to pinpoint his aggressor. "Damn! Where the hell is he!" Flushed with anger at himself for not handling this fiasco sooner, he ambled to the stairs leading to the street, but sprinted the five blocks to fight the chilly night air.

As he turned the key to his door, his eyes caught a dark figure walking in his direction some distance away. Blake rushed through the foyer and entered his livingroom. He opened the window blind facing the street and kept the room dark. As the figure approached, hunched up to fight the chill, Blake squinted his eyes for a better view but poor street lighting prevented any attempt at identification.

The dark figure, now at Blake's property, hesitated a few seconds, did an about face and retraced his steps in the direction of the railroad station. Blake, now at his wit's end, quickly left his place and followed not ten yards behind. The figure, aware of Blake's presence, continued on his way and soon re-entered the station waiting room. Blake peered past a window rim to see the same face that brought about the loathing he felt some hours before. Infuriated, and almost maniacally, drawing his small pistol, he stormed into the waiting room and faced his oppressor.

"Who the hell are you and what the hell are you doing here?"

Without raising himself from his seat and without any apparent fear of the weapon, he faced Blake. "My name is Juan Lopez, I am the brother of Maria Lopez, the beautiful woman you murdered. You're the last of the five persons of interest. The other four have been cleared. Although a longshot, I've convinced the local authorities that you are the murderer. I riled you these past hours to get you to follow me here, at this late hour; to this out-of-the-way place, to hear your confession."

Flushed with revenge for all he endured, Blake erupted. He bent over the seated Juan, grabbed his throat and pointed the gun barrel at Juan's brow.

"I've had enough of you, you son-of-a-bitch. Yeah, I did it, and now it's your turn."

Without warning, the chief of detectives and three deputies, weapons drawn, burst in.

"Okay! Okay! Drop the gun! Now!"

Blake was stunned for the moment but didn't draw his pistol from Juan's brow. He turned his head slightly to determine if the officers, in fact, had him cornered. Then, in a split second, forced Juan to stand with his back to the officers, using him as a shield.

"I'm warning you, don't try anything stupid. This place is surrounded. If you want to make it out of here alive, you'd better drop it."

In an act of defiance, with the pistol still at his brow, Juan, now eye to eye with Blake, "If you take me out, you're dead too." With an unsteady trigger finger and confronted with four pieces of artillery aimed at him, Blake finally lowered his pistol.

The modus operandi based on a psychological approach was eminently successful but a hand-cuffed Blake was not impressed. Almost berserk, "I'll get you yet, I'll get you yet," Blake ranted as he was led to a nearby squadcar.

"Did you record his confession?" asked one of the deputies.

Juan, feeling for the wire the police had secreted on his person, "Yeah, I got it."

SNAPSHOT

❖ ❖ ❖ ❖ ❖ ❖ ❖ ❖

"Oh my god! Look at my face!"

Norma's mirror revealed horrid red blotches and swelling.

"I told you to check the risks before you used that skin cream", admonished her mother. They always list them on the carton. You'll never listen to me."

Norma's visit to a dermatologist confirmed that her condition was the result of the application. "I'm going to sue that damn pharmaceutical company! They can't do this to me!"

"Ask dad to take photos of your face. You'll need evidence if you sue. You never know if the condition won't clear up quickly. Even by tomorrow. Get him to take pictures now. Sid, where's that old camera we used in Italy last year?" asked Lena.

"It's in the top closet," said Sid. "I'll get it."

"You'll need film."

"There's still some left from our trip to Italy."

The mention of Italy dismissed the immediacy of Norma's problem and was replaced by Sid's and Lena's nostalgic thoughts of the Sistene Chapel in Rome, the statue of 'David' in Florence, shopping in Milan, fishdinners in Naples, and Venician gondolas.

Then nostalgia to reality. "Hey, dad! How about photos of my face. That's more important than your trip to Italy. That was a year ago. This is now!'

"OK! OK! Let's go!"

Sid set up his tripod to insure sharp images of the awful blotches. Norma posed statue-like and looked directly into the camera aperture. Snap! Nothing happened. Snap! Same result.

"Let's trade places so I can see for myself if the aperture is working properly." Sid examined the aperture as Norma snapped the shutter.

"Seems to be working fine."

Each returned to their former positions and continued to the end of the roll.

After a few days, Norma was ecstatic. Her blemishes miraculously disappeared and she had photographs taken to prove her case.

Sid arrived home. Norma tore open the photo packet. All of the photos showed areas of unexposed film except for a great shot of Sid, glasses balanced on his brow and an inquisitive expression on his face along with a spectacular photo of the leaning tower of Pisa.

OUR SECRET FOREVER

❖ ❖ ❖ ❖ ❖ ❖ ❖ ❖ ❖ ❖ ❖ ❖ ❖ ❖ ❖ ❖ ❖ ❖ ❖ ❖

In the first world war, more soldiers perished from the Influenza pandemic than from battle injuries. During that same period, Jenny, my father's first wife, along with many of the world's population, died from that same devastating disease.

When Jenny was alive, her young sister, Pauline, was always there to baby sit for Jenny's two young children, Irving, age five and Pearl, nearing her first birthday.

After Jenny's passing, Pauline, because of her baby sitting, devotion to the children and fondness for the children's father, Willie, was asked by her mother if she would consider marrying Willie. After all, who would be more attentive to the children than Pauline. Wouldn't a stranger marrying Willie also be a stranger to the children? Wouldn't it be best for Pauline to marry Willie?

Pauline, the youngest in a family of eight children, immediately turned down her mother's will, along with her siblings who vehemently disapproved. After all, Willie was thirty six years old with two young children and Pauline was a young, naive, sixteen!

Nevertheless, after long, contentious family meetings, and after thoughtful consideration of her love for her sister and the children, Pauline finally acceded to her mother's wishes. Although not the best way to enter a marriage of uncertainty, she would make the best of it.

Over the years very little or nothing was discussed about the marriage arrangement for Willie's new family. Only Irving, at five years when the new marriage occurred, was old enough to remember his mother. It was true but hard to accept, as he got older, Irving's unrevealing of the circumstances that gave rise to that new family structure. Could it have been because of his feeling comfortable in the presence of his once baby sitter? And Pearl, from a very young age, had no reason to believe that Pauline was not her mother

Years passed. Three children were added to the brood. Pearl accepted her new brother and sisters, as they were born, as normal additions to a natural family. Incredibly, at the ripe age of twenty-four, my mother, Pauline, was now with the responsibly of five children.

Irving, the eldest, was always there to help his step-mother in many ways. In my conversations with him, I always felt he was aware and appreciated what she endured and accepted her as his real mother.

Willie, I'm sure, was always mindful of the fact that Pauline was there to make his family whole, once again. So, fortunate to have sufficient resources, he hired sleep-in maids, over the years, to help Pauline clean a large home, prepare dinner and care for the younger children and as the family progressed, so did Pauline's adjustment to her age difference with Willie. Even her siblings had softened their resentment.

And the time came when we felt comfortable, as a normal family, going about our business as other families did until we were confronted with some distressing news.

At age thirteen, my sister Ethel was to endure major surgery. Discussion with a medical team regarding comparative blood types for transfusion from family members, was necessary for her recovery. As a result, the family secret was finally revealed! The only member of the family not present at the hospital at that moment, my father was not aware of the startling revelation that his children were finally informed of the fact that they were composed of step brothers and sisters. Nor was he ever aware. It was obvious to all of us that he was content with the family makeup. And so, we, the children of Willie and Pauline, after emotional discussions, and considering the obvious pledge he made to himself to keep the family makeup not a topic of conversation, for whatever reason, decided that it was to be our secret too, forever.

To this day, regardless of the explosive knowledge gained at the hospital so long ago, have always, nevertheless, regarded ourselves as true brothers and sisters, all having had one mother and one father.

I once asked my mother if she ever loved my father. "Your father always was a gracious, caring, thoughtful man who worked hard to give us the best of everything. I have no regrets."

My parents, Pauline and Willie are no longer with us, our secret buried with him. In my family album I have a treasured photograph of them, at advanced age, in a close embrace, smiling… and holding hands.

IN RETROSPECT

❖ ❖ ❖ ❖ ❖ ❖ ❖ ❖ ❖ ❖ ❖ ❖ ❖ ❖

He felt fortunate. The patient in the hospital bed adjacent to his seemed reasonable, amiable and with a good sense of humor, things you don't ordinarily find in someone just hours after returning from being in the hands of a surgeon.

"So how did it go?" he asked.

"I'm still here. What more can I say," answered his newly acquired friend.

"Was the surgery really necessary?"

"Oh, absolutely! In the second world war, it must be at least seventy years ago, a bullet pierced some muscle and nerves just above my knee and the military docs sort of patched it together at a surgery station in a medical outpost. It really didn't heal properly and over the years I tolerated the discomfort until recently when I decided to do something about it. So here I am. What are you here for?"

"You won't believe this. I'm here for a battlefield wound too, from the same war. During a devastating attack on our unit, I took several slivers of shrapnel in my back. Recently I began to feel pain in that same area and a MRI revealed two slivers still embedded there."

"How did your surgery go?"

"OK for now. Hopefully the discomfort will be gone."

"By the way, where were you stationed?"

"I was in China in a supply unit delivering ammunition to our front lines."

"This is incredible. I was in China too. And would you believe me if I told you my mission was basically the same except that my unit delivered supplies to the medics in the field?"

"So here we are, together after so many years, with somewhat the same mission and with battle wounds being repaired, in the same room in a hospital with one hundred fifty beds. thousands of miles from those struggles. Incredible."

"When are you scheduled for rehab?"

"Probably not for two or three days."

"I feel pretty good. The doc told me I'll be in there tomorrow."

"Good. We'll meet there. I'm sure we'll have some interesting battle experiences to talk about."

Days later, during a rehab rest period, "You know, in the years since the end of WWII, I never felt comfortable talking about my experiences on the battlefield. Not even to my family, but for you as a vet, I'll try."

With his palm covering his lips, his eyes closed, his shoulders bent, the entire episode passed quickly through his mind. After some seconds, "In Lanzhou, northern China, a shell exploded within yards of my position with shrapnel tearing into my back and lacerating areas of my leg. I must have been unconscious for awhile and when I awoke I was on a stretcher being carried to a rescue helicopter when another shell burst almost on top of us, totaling the copter and throwing me and the bearers several feet in the air. Unfortunately, only one bearer and I survived. Hours later another copter landed and in the midst and chaos of exploding shells, I was eventually evacuated along with several other wounded. It was a rough time."

"I know what you're saying. Those times were rough for me too." Then, with pursed lips, his eyes riveted on the doctors and nurses passing beyond the open door of his room. he soon began, slowly at first. "I remember it was on a dusky evening with street fighting in Tianjin, with our troops pursuing the enemy through darkened alleys. I was trying to keep up with my supplying small ammunition when I got one in the leg. Even with all hell breaking loose I was able to tie a tourniquet with a heavy cord from some equipment I was carrying. Several hours later, somehow, I found myself in a tent hospital with a medic captain tending my wound. He told me I was lucky. Without the tourniquet, and no medic present, I could have bled to death."

After a long pause… "You know, it wasn't a good idea to be friendly with another guy in your outfit. I remember a recruit from basic training who came along with me all the way. The last time I saw him, half his face was gone."

"Pretty grim but there were other battle areas that were far worse than China where we were. I think that fierce engagement on Iwo Jima was the bloodiest of them all. I understand that one of our guys was killed every minute and a half."

"I never knew that but I feel that all were the bloodiest. That first engagement on Guadalcanal was no picnic and, of course, Burma was near the top of the list with more blood than jungle foliage."

"You know, on rare occasions when conversation about the war comes up, I keep thinking of my two childhood friends who didn't survive that slaughterhouse on New Guinea,"

All at once, a wall of silence shut out all talk about war with both sets of eyes concentrating on imaginary spots on the tiled ceiling.

Then…getting back to reality, "By the way, who's handling your rehab?"

"Molly, the pretty one in the corner by the window."

"She supervises my rehab too. Incidentally, she told me she's getting married."

Molly, a middle-aged female supply sergeant in the Vietnam encounter, after being together with her patients for a period of two weeks, bonded with them. They were all veterans and veterans always thought of themselves as one family no matter where they came from.

On a whim, "Say how would you guys like to come to my wedding? Very few guests. It will take place in my sister's beautiful back yard. And I'm sure Donald, my future, won't mind. Please, I'd like to see you there."

Of course they would come.

One invitation was addressed to Robert O'Neil.

Another invitation was addressed to his long ago enemy, Ichiro Nakamura.

OUR NEIGHBOR TO THE RIGHT

❖❖❖❖❖❖❖❖❖❖❖❖❖❖❖❖❖❖❖❖❖❖❖❖❖❖

Zimmerstein, flushed with anger, was showing a congregation of empathetic neighbors where his garden sprinkler hose was severed about twelve inches from the faucet spout. I pulled on to my driveway, shut the engine, stiffened my arms against the steering wheel, pushing my shoulders into the back of the seat, and stared at the animated gathering. My presence brought looks of suspicion but as I left the car and neared the group, they opened a path almost as an invitation for me to examine the useless hose. "Who could have done such a dastardly thing?", someone asked looking squarely at me. I looked squarely back and shrugged my shoulders with a how-should-I know gesture.

No, it couldn't be…my wife didn't have the strength to do that kind of cutting, and besides, it was surgically accurate. Yet, as I looked up and caught an almost silhouetted Elaine viewing the scene below, the expression she wore told me otherwise.

We met the Zimmersteins sometime after the concrete was poured for the sidewalks along our elegantly curved street, Oak Drive.

"Hi! This your new home?"

"Yep."

"Roz and Rick Zimmerstein", he introduced himself and his wife. "That's our place.", pointing to the foundation immediately to the right of us. "Looks like we're going to be next door neighbors."

And so they were. This gracious young couple, not long after the last piece of furniture was moved were somehow transformed. They became warriors, hiding being their castle walls and engaging their perceived enemy, us, in battle. despite the fact there was never any declaration of war.

Construction was completed that Fall and moving vans dotted the community. The Zimmersteins were already settled when we turned the key to our new place. That evening they graciously welcomed us and we spent a few hours talking about the school tax, real estate tax, commutation cost and an upcoming railroad strike, local sales tax and the like. Nevertheless, a pleasant evening.

Winter brought neighborly small talk from behind snow shovels and common complaints when the county plows spilled mountains of snow in front of everyone's driveway. Not long after, car trunks were loaded with everything from fertilizer spreaders and weed and crabgrass killers, to garden hoses and balled shrubbery with little white tags holding names like Ilex Aquifolium, Taxus Cuspidata and Tsuga Canadensis, definitions of which were unknown to those with 'A' grades in high school Latin.

On a beautiful sunny day, almost destroyed by an annoying railroad slowdown, I relaxed with some hot coffee from our company kitchen. I was thinking how enjoyable it would be tackling the weeds already sprouting in the shrub beds when my phone rang disrupting that pleasant thought.

"Jane's new bedroom carpeting is soaking wet. Know what from?" asked Elaine. "It's that idiot Roz. Her sprinkler is throwing water as high as our second floor. When I called her to let her know, she told me to close the window! I already did that before I called. Can you believe the stupidity? It better not happen tomorrow!"

"I don't think it was intentional. She probably doesn't know how to set the controls. I'm sure it won't happen again." My logic didn't soften Elaine's rage. "Like I said. It better not happen tomorrow!"

The next morning, getting myself more comfortable in my office chair, the desk phone rang. I sensed immediately that Roz had repeated her deed. Elaine, seething, offered confirmation. "She turns the damn sprinkler on as soon as your car pulls away."

"Okay...Okay! Tomorrow I'll drive around the block and return. Then we'll see what's what."

As I expected, there was Roz walking towards the front door, quickening her pace as she saw my car approach; the sprinkler splattering our second floor window. In her haste, she tripped over the hose, raised and collected herself from all fours and continued to her front door. "Roz! Can I speak to you for a moment?" Pretending not to hear, she closed the door behind her.

Parking at her curb, I raced up the flagstone walk and rang her bell. No response. After several minutes of intermittent bell ringing, I decided to confront Rick with the problem. The vicious growling of Helmut, Roz's elephant-sized German Shepherd, although leashed to a Weeping Cherry Tree, was also a factor in my decision.

I called Rick that evening. He declined to meet me for a walk around the neighborhood, obviously aware of his wife's indiscreet use of the sprinkler and didn't want to discuss it for whatever reason.

For a period of two weeks the problem was not with us. It had accompanied the Zimmersteins on their vacation. When they returned so did the sprinkler, but in a more devastating manner.

On Monday, July 15th, 7:30 A.M., Dean, our nine-month-old son was asleep in his stroller in our backyard screened porch. His loud bawling brought Elaine there. She was greeted by a scene reminiscent of the great flood. Zimmerstein's rotating sprinkler, placed close to our fence line, was cascading onto the porch totally saturating the stroller, the pillow, the sheet and most important...Dean!

Livid, Elaine brought the baby into the house, made him comfortable and quickly returned to the porch. Opening the screen door, she accelerated the sixteen feet of lawn and cleared the cowrail fence onto Zimmerstein's property with a leap that would have been the envy of an olympic hurdler. Drenching herself before she could gain control of the spray, she folded the hose at a strategic distance and picked up the sprinkler. Utterly disregarding the untethered Helmut's exposed fangs and low menacing growl, she scrambled up the back steps, opened the kitchen door and examined the premises. "Where was the precise center of the room to get the greatest concentration of splash?" she thought quickly. Elaine placed the sprinkler in the selected spot and undid the bent hose, allowing the water to surge into the sprinkler. This immediately triggered the rotator, releasing a deluge comparable to an Asiatic monsoon, inundating every square inch of he kitchen. Having accomplished her goal and standing not three feet from the sprinkler in her wringing wet, clinging, translucent nightgown, her hair plastered, and with hands on hips and in a slightly bent forward posture, inquired in a fiery voice, "How do you like that Zimmerstein?"

Roz, scurrying up from the basement laundry room to investigate, arrived just as the question was being posed. Stunned by the scene of her sopping wet kitchen and the rotator still splashing Elaine, her response was a resounding, "H-O-L-Y S _ _ T. After several Summers and some minor irritations (Roz never completely learned) a peek through our living room blinds revealed a moving van backing onto Zimmerstein, s driveway. Our prayers were answered.

In a welcoming gesture, we invited our new neighbors, Fred and Amy, to spend their first evening with us. For a few hours we discussed the school tax, real estate tax, commutation cost and an upcoming railroad strike, local tax and the like. Nevertheless, a pleasant evening. Fred, pausing before leaving asked, "Oh, by the way, Larry, I'm planning to install an underground sprinkler. I understand water waste is minimal if the spray heads are faced into my property. Is that true?"

I bubbled. A man after my own heart. "That's true Fred... absolutely true."

NEIGHBORHOOD HAPPENING

Irving Borsuck was furious. The punk! punk! punk! heard from the outside wall of his pharmacy by those pesky neighborhood kids playing handball, had begun to unnerve him. They had better beware if they think handball playing on the wall of his business will forever be tolerated.

Those pesky kids were unshaken by his threats, resolute in their determination to continue their daily rounds of handball playing. They had no choice. Considering all possibilities, there was no other place in the surrounding vicinity, not even in the nearby schoolyard, where space could easily be adapted to the dimensions of a handball court.

Irving Borsuck was also resolute. In an act of defiance, before entering his pharmacy each morning, he would maneuver his English minicar onto a calculated center of the handball court, for his daily parking.

Fury was now in the camp of the handball players.

To Irving Borsuck's dismay, after several days of parking, six of those pesky handball players settled behind areas of his minicar and with great heft, relocated it near the curb facing the entrance to the pharmacy.

Seething, and with a more severe threat, Irving Borsuck contacted the local police who visited each family of those pesky handball players, with an appropriate lecture.

The visitations were successful. Irving Borsuck no longer had to contend with the punk! punk! punk! from the outside wall of his pharmacy.

Disgruntled and in an act of bravado, those pesky kids congregated daily on the vacated handball court to demonstrate their resentment.

Then it happened! Smoke billowed from the entrance of the pharmacy. Four of those pesky kids rushed through the acrid smoke to find Irving Borsuck lying on the floor of his office. They lifted him by his hands and feet and carried him through the flames now gutting the pharmacy area. Once outside, they sat him against the wall of the once used handball court. One of those pesky kids removed his sweater as a pillow to rest his head. Others raced to a nearby Pizzeria and called 911. Another sprinted to a doctor's office he knew nearby.

As a large crowd gathered, those pesky kids convinced one of the neighbors to rush to her home and provide a blanket to be placed on the unconscious pharmacist.

In short order, police and fire department personnel arrived along with a medical team. The pesky kids helped police cordon off the area to keep the curious from hindering their efforts.

Irving Borsuck was resuscitated but required hospitalization.

Tears welled in his eyes as he received those pesky kids who surrounded his hospital bed, each expressing their hope that he soon return to his pharmacy.

Not long after, Irving Borsuck was seen, along with those pesky kids, painting the white stripes of a professional handball court on the wall of his pharmacy.

All to the applause of the nearby neighbors.

PICKPOCKET

❖ ❖ ❖ ❖ ❖ ❖ ❖ ❖ ❖ ❖ ❖

An elderly rider was holding the ceiling strap to steady himself in the heavily crowded crosstown bus. This caused the lapel of his unbuttoned jacket to fall away, revealing what appeared to be a wallet, or money folder, in his exposed shirt pocket. A rather well-attired young man pushing through the crowd, positioned himself between his potential pickpocket victim and Marty; in effect three bodies with no room to spare.

His face inches from the victim's, the pickpocket waited for the precise opportunity to present itself. Despite his awareness of Marty's close presence and using the arm that held the ceiling strap as a shield, he would make several attempts to reach for the shirt pocket's contents only to pull back each time as the victim adjusted his position in an attempt to comfort himself in the tight squeeze. After several attempts with deft use of his fingers, success was accomplished. The empty shirt pocket no longer held what obviously was of value to the victim; a telephone number, a few dollars of pocket money, or whatever, along with a later feeling of guilt for having allowed this degrading of his person.

Marty's proximity allowed him to observe the entire episode but he decided to take no action to thwart the pickpocket's intentions which could have resulted in a violent reaction from him and possible injuries to the crowded passengers.

"Next stop 54th Street," bellowed the bus driver.

Being the closest to the midway exit, Marty reached over the stairwell to push open the doors. Suddenly, and without excusing herself, a young lady positioned herself between Marty and the doors and pretended to having a problem with them. Being a gentleman, he bent over her in an effort to assist. While still bent over her, she pushed her butt against him, forcing him into the crowd behind. At that moment, and to his utter resentment, someone attempted to dislodge the wallet from his back pocket.

Incensed, and immediately aware that this was a concerted effort by the two participants, Marty used his knee in a forward thrust against the butt of this bent over figure, flinging her headfirst past the stairwell and on to the concrete sidewalk.

As the midday strollers stopped to stare, Marty coolly stepped down on to the stairwell and leaped over her body which exhibited some traces of scrapes and bruises. Her accomplice, obviously not satisfied with his initial success, followed him through the exit and helped her to her feet. The bus driver, unaware of the occurrence, closed the doors and continued on his route.

To his amazement, no reaction followed but as Marty left the scene and walked past the store windows lining the avenue, he became aware that he was being followed by the two. Stopping at one window and pretending to observe a clothing display, he was able to use the window's reflections to observe their movements, along with their side glances, as they paraded past him and turned the corner at the end of the street. The commotion at the bus stop alerted a nearby patrolman who approached Mark after pointing him out by one of the spectators at the scene.

After a double-quick accounting of the recent events, Marty and the patrolman raced around the corner and after a short chase and brief struggle, managed to handcuff the pickpocket. During this scuffle, the female accomplice was able to flee but Marty, together with the assist of two young men who witnessed the event, eventually cornered her.

Waiting for the police van to escort the pair to police headquarters, Marty used the time to retaliate for the attempt by the perpetrators to remove the wallet from his back pocket. He approached the two, now forced to sit on the pavement, opening his wallet wide to show it held no cash and nothing of value for the pickpocket.

As the two were escorted to the police van, Marty, with a sarcastic grin that reached both ears, thrust his fist at them, his erect index finger pointing skyward.